The
Way
to Stay
in
Destiny

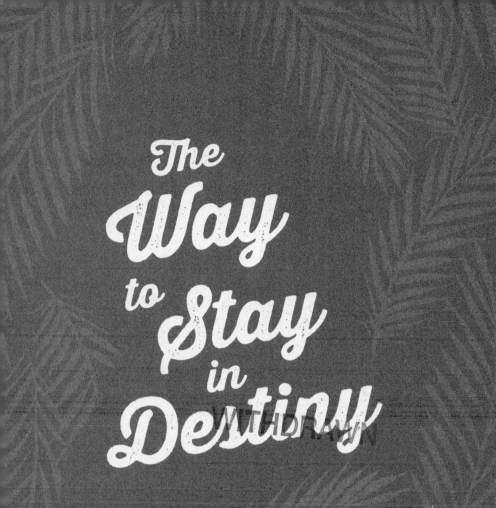

The Way to Stay in Destiny

AUGUSTA SCATTERGOOD

SCHOLASTIC PRESS | NEW YORK

Library of Congress Cataloging-in-Publication Data available

ISBN 978-0-545-53824-4

10 9 8 7 6 5 4 3 2 1   15 16 17 18 19

Printed in the U.S.A.   23
First edition, January 2015

Book design by Elizabeth B. Parisi

FOR DR. JACK RUSSEL,
WHO INSPIRED HIS CHILDREN WITH STORIES.
AND FOR MY BROTHER, JACK,
WHO KEEPS THEM ALIVE.

CHAPTER ONE

Welcome to Destiny

The crazy lady in seat 2B hasn't stopped singing "You Are My Sunshine" since the glare hit the windshield three hours ago. Okay, maybe I nodded off for a minute or two. And maybe that's a line of drool on my chin. But when my uncle punches me in the arm, hard, I jump wide awake.

"Get off the bus, Theo," Uncle Raymond says, pushing ahead of a girl moving too slow for him. "We're in Destiny."

I grab my bags and baseball glove and follow him.

The minute the door opens, heat hits me like a slap in the face. When a whoosh of diesel fumes almost knocks me over, I hold my breath and step onto the blazing sidewalk.

Everywhere, old men wearing shorts, flip-flops, and big smiles grab suitcases. They hug relatives and hustle them off in station wagons. But nobody's expecting us at this Marathon Gas Station.

Wait a minute. What's all that slithery gray stuff hanging from the trees? I kick at two brown coconuts littering the ground, squint up at the sinking sun, and shake my head at the banner swinging from one streetlight across to another: *Welcome to Destiny, Florida, the Town Time Forgot.*

Leaning down to pick up my knapsack, I jerk it away when a tiny lizard skitters under a plant so sharp it could cut off my fingers. I push up the long, hot sleeves of the shirt that was just fine when we left Kentucky early yesterday, and all I can think is *Oh man. What am I doing here?*

One good thing — I'm tossing the jacket I've been sleeping on. It stinks worse than my granddaddy's hog pen. Not to mention my arms don't hardly fit in the sleeves anymore.

I dangle the coat over a trash can on the sidewalk. "Too hot for this," I say.

Uncle Raymond swats at my jacket. "Keep it," he growls. "Just in case."

I jam the coat in my bag. Wondering what *just in case* could ever need a puke-green jacket like mine.

My uncle puts his big tool chest down, unfolds a piece of paper, and nods toward a flowery row of bushes. "Turn down there. Miss Grandersole says her Rest Easy Rooming House is off Main Street."

He shoves the note in my hand and leaves me on the corner. While he stops to stare at a statue of some old army guy on the town square, I spot the Chat 'n' Chew Cafe. Next door's an ice-cream stand! Actual kids eating Popsicles and looking normal. My stomach rumbles at the smell of greasy hot dogs frying and the thought of an orange sno-cone.

I hurry to catch up with my uncle. "Wanna get something to eat?" I ask.

"Supper's included with our room," he barks out, then keeps walking.

I wipe the sweat off my eyebrows and look up at a tree thick with leaves. A zillion green birds blink down from a high branch. Whoa! A green bird? Not in a cage? I jump backward. No way am I standing under a flock of pooping birds.

I try to raise my voice above their squawking. "Wait up, Uncle Raymond! You said this was a beach town. Where's the ocean?"

"Don't you know nothing? It ain't no ocean. It's the Gulf of Mexico. I got no time for dawdling. Gotta get ready for my new job tomorrow." Uncle Raymond shoots a big rock off the sidewalk with his heavy work boots. "Keep up," he hollers.

I uncrumple the note he shoved in my hand.

1. *Turn left at the stoplight.*

2. *Go two blocks down Breezy Way Street.*

3. *Rest Easy Rooming House is on your right, just after the live oak tree.*

Sure that I'm being chased by green birds, I scoop up my suitcase just as a loud rumble of thunder shakes the sidewalk under me.

Really, things can't get much worse in Destiny.

CHAPTER TWO

Living at the Rest Easy

*I*nstead of begging to climb back on the bus and keep riding till we get someplace as cool and normal as the mountains we left, I follow my uncle. We turn the corner onto a street of square houses lined up like Monopoly pieces and stop at the biggest, with a porch wrapped around three sides. I read the sign:

Miss Sister Grandersole's Rest Easy
Rooming House and Dance Academy

"'Dance Academy'? Nobody said we'd be living at a *dance academy*." I glare at my uncle. He shrugs and stomps up the stairs.

Ignoring June bugs buzzing the porch light, I notice the sign's been spruced up with a big pot of my grandma's favorite flowers. She plants those red geraniums close to her toma-toes. Make that *planted*. Guess she's not worrying about flowers and tomatoes at the nursing home back in Kentucky.

Uncle Raymond leans in close to the window, checking his reflection, touching his shirt to be sure it's buttoned way up under his neck. He looks again, then takes two steps back. "Folks inside eating," he says. "We'll come back later."

Maybe *he* thinks the people passing mashed potatoes around that supper table don't want to be disturbed, but my stomach's still rumbling, and now it's starting to rain. Pushing aside two pillows decorated with the same sayings Grandma stitched and framed all over the farmhouse, I slump down on the porch glider.

"I'm hungry." I cross my arms, daring my uncle to leave.

Just as Uncle Raymond turns away, a lady wearing a long flowery skirt swings open the front door. "My stars! You must be Mr. Raymond Gary." When she sweeps her hand back, about a zillion bracelets jangle, and I jump up. "And Theo. Look at you. What a tall, handsome boy!"

I can't help it. I smile real big at this lady. Uncle Raymond nods and picks up his heavy tool chest and his old army duf-fel. We follow her inside.

"Call me Miss Sister. Everybody does." Her eyes crinkle up in that way that means she's really glad we're here. "Welcome to my home. Mrs. Hernandez cooked a special supper for our new guests."

Good thing I passed up hot dogs at the Chat 'n' Chew. Fried chicken, biscuits, and those mashed potatoes are piled high. Best meal since my grandmother got too sick to cook almost two years ago.

Before I lick the last taste of peach cobbler off my spoon, Miss Sister's already leading us upstairs, pointing at the pictures lining her hallway.

"My dance recitals, Theo. I offer tap and ballet every Wednesday afternoon and on Saturdays." She sways a little, flutters her fingers. "Why, you are going to love it here. There's the ice-cream stand downtown. The Clearview Cinema picture show. And of course, the beach. Have you seen the beach?" She looks back at me. "Nice little place, Destiny. Next month we'll celebrate the town's birthday. June 11, 1974 — Destiny will be one hundred years old!"

My granddaddy's farm was older than that, but I keep my mouth shut.

Miss Sister keeps talking, with me and my uncle walking close behind her. "Lots going on. My dance recital. Baseball all summer. You play baseball, don't you, honey?"

Maybe I don't know anything about beaches, but I was All-County shortstop before Uncle Raymond took over.

Then Miss Sister's talking again and moving fast. I pretty much have to jog to keep up.

In the upstairs hall, I catch a deep breath of lemon furniture polish, and a frayed carpet edge almost trips me up. Of course, that's exactly when a girl with hair like a family of garter snakes sunning themselves on her head bounces out. I catch my balance and smile. The girl does not smile back.

"Hope you enjoy your stay," Miss Sister's saying. "Mamie here — she and her mother have been living at the Rest Easy since Mamie was a little bit of a thing, and here she's about to turn six."

The skinny girl scrunches up her mouth and points. "I heard you were coming. Hope y'all don't make a lot of noise 'cause my mama needs her beauty sleep. She's studying hair and makeup over at the Mister Tony's Institute and Hairdresser School. She practices on me." Mamie flips her snake curls around, sticks her tongue out, and disappears into what I guess is her room.

Miss Sister rolls her eyes. "Don't pay too much attention to that child," she whispers, then laughs. "*If* you can help it!" She opens the door across from Mamie's. "One of my bigger rooms! Make yourselves real comfortable. I'll see you at breakfast," and she's down the stairs.

Frilly white curtains almost cover the air conditioner humming away in a window. Two beds, one just longer than the other, a sink, a tall bureau. I walk across to the closet and drop my knapsack. I turn to the shorter bed in the corner, running my hand across the smooth blue blanket and fat pillow. Let my uncle claim the bed that's big enough for his long legs. Maybe he'll stop complaining about his bum knee. Over my bed, there's a radio on the shelf.

Uncle Raymond opens the window and takes deep breaths, leaning out like he's trying to escape. "Not nearly the same as the night sky in Alaska," he says. Without even looking at me, he mumbles, "And this here rooming house is a fancy hotel compared to my little cabin up there."

I bite my tongue so as not to blurt out that this room we're sharing's not half as big as my room at the farm. And the sky Granddaddy and me looked at most every night? Probably prettier than what Uncle Raymond's always blabbing about seeing in Alaska.

Before I can turn around good, my uncle steps back and starts arranging his undershirts and socks in drawers. He tosses the rest on the closet floor.

"Those are dirty. Tomorrow's Saturday. Find a Laundromat."

On the bus ride from Kentucky, my uncle laid out the rules. Yep, I'll be Washing the Clothes — every Saturday from now until I'm old enough not to have Uncle Raymond bossing me around.

When I reach down to pick up his dirty undershirt, my leather bracelet slips out from my long shirtsleeve. I twist it, fiddling with the snap.

"What's that?" My uncle's staring at my wrist.

I hold it up. "Made this with my best friend back in Kentucky," I say.

"Take that sissified thing off." He jams another shirt into a drawer. "Get rid of it."

"Granddaddy didn't mind." I push the band farther up my arm, out of sight.

"Things are different now." My uncle pounds a fist into his palm, over and over while he paces around the room. "Just me and you. You got to follow my rules."

"Yessir," I whisper, backing away. I line up my baseball glove and my tattered book, *Everything You Want to Know about Baseball Players*, on the windowsill above my bed.

I don't hardly have time to unpack my shorts and jeans. Or put away the fat envelope of school records and other important stuff before Uncle Raymond's pulling on the ceiling fan cord to cut out the light. Across the darkness of the room, he says, "Little girl next door's trouble. Don't go sharing our business around here."

"I plan to stay as far away from Mamie as I can get," I answer. But my uncle's snoring is already starting up.

Then, just when I'm drifting off to sleep, I hear something. Music! Ignoring Uncle Raymond tossing and calling out with a nightmare, I slip into the hall. A door opens, then closes softly. Mamie, snooping. Forget about her. There's a piano somewhere, and I'm holding my breath listening.

Exactly two weeks ago, May 3, 1974, I was playing "Happy Birthday" to my grandmother on our rickety living room piano. By then, she didn't remember much. But she sang all the words to that song. And while I was trying to act like it was fine and dandy that my uncle was dragging me away, Granddaddy was bawling his eyes out.

That was the last time I touched a piano key.

My grandparents' farm? Sold. The old piano went wherever the furniture ended up. And me? Theo M. Thomas? Previously destined to be a famous musician or maybe a big leaguer? I packed my entire life in a suitcase and a knapsack and pretended the uncle I'd never laid eyes on wasn't swearing we'd never set foot in Kentucky again.

Hearing the music drift up the stairs, I grab the hall banister tight. Every single note waltzes straight to my insides and makes me want to play along.

Okay, so I've left behind my friends, my grandparents, and the farm I'd lived on pretty much all my life. My new room's above a tap-dance studio and next door to a five-year-old pain in the butt. What's worse, an uncle I don't hardly know speaks to me mostly when he's barking out orders.

But before tiptoeing back down the dark hall, I've decided there's one good thing about being hauled off to Destiny, Florida. Tomorrow I'll find that piano.

CHAPTER THREE

No Piano Playing Ever

The next morning, before the first ray of sunlight beams through the bedroom curtains, I slide my feet out of the covers and inch across the floor. I stumble over dirty high-tops, exactly where I kicked them last night. When Uncle Raymond rolls over, snoring like a freight train, I slip my shorts on. Grabbing my T-shirt off the chair, I creep down the hall.

Downstairs, a door that was shut last night is still closed. But the glass doorknob turns pretty easy. Two deep breaths. Step inside. Shut the door, real quiet.

Wow. I'm looking at the biggest, shiniest piano, smooth and silent in the back of the room. No furniture except a couple of folding chairs in the corner. Mirrors everywhere. This must be the dance studio.

Sitting on the bench, I open up the piano and run my hands

up the keyboard. Oh man, every note's perfect! Turning from side to side, I wink at the zillion faces staring back from the mirrors lining the walls. Faces with dark brown eyes and curly brown hair. All mine.

Hey, you! Wearing a silver sequined suit like that Elvis guy! Girls swooning! Theo Thomas, Piano Player to the Stars. Theo, baby! Whatcha gonna play for us today?

Who's stopping me? I tap another white key, real quiet. Then a black one. I make up a melody on the high notes, soft and slow. I play it again. Faster. While the music's in my head, I forget the room, the day, even my uncle. I'm so busy dreaming up melodies, I'm lost inside the big piano.

So I don't hear the heavy studio door bang open.

"Theo? Boy, is that you?" My uncle drops his tool chest hard on the shiny waxed floor. He storms toward the piano. Faster than I can move, he slams the keyboard cover hard on top of my hands. Not letting on how much that hurt, I stand up and jam my fists into my pockets.

"What're you doing in here?" he says, so mean and quiet I have to lean in to hear.

"Haven't played since Granddaddy's," I answer, fighting back tears, squeezing my fingers open and shut. "I'm not bothering anybody."

Uncle Raymond bangs his fist down on the shiny piano, then pulls it back as if it's burning hot. "Git away from that thing. Right now. It don't belong to you."

"Can I ask that Miss Sister lady if it's okay? I bet it's her piano."

"Nobody but a fool wastes time on music. I told you when we left the farm, we ain't got time for foolishness."

I look hard at my uncle's straight-as-an-arrow side part, every single hair in place, hair tonic stinking to high heaven. I stare into those mean black eyes to send him a message. If I touch a key or two, fast and jazzy, if I stretch my sneakers onto those pedal things, maybe then the music will make my uncle smile.

Fat chance.

He turns away, still spitting mad. "Can't be bothering about this. Got to get to work. My old army buddy, he got me this job. Boss is coming in early to show me the ropes. Least there's somebody left who appreciates what we both fought for." Uncle Raymond turns and narrows his eyes. "You need something, ask Miss Grandersole. Be polite about it." He jabs his finger toward the piano. "Don't ask her about that thing," he says, and storms out the door.

I listen for his heavy boots to clunk down the front porch

steps. One-two-three. Then nothing. Good. He's gone. Wait four more beats, then open the piano.

When I finally stop playing, my fingers ache. I rub them together and squeeze my eyes shut. A deep breath of musty music books lined up on the dance studio shelf makes me remember a different piano, almost as big as this, a bench full of sheet music. Way back. Me climbing in a lap and touching soft hands moving up and down the keys.

I play real quiet till the big door opens again and I jump, praying it's not Uncle Raymond come back. Instead, shiny black shoes click-click across the floor. Miss Sister does a little twirl with her hands spread out and her red hair swirling every which way. "Why, my lands, Theo, you play the piano! Beautiful!"

"Just tunes I make up. I can't read music too good." I rub the polished black wood, and I don't close the keyboard cover. "Never saw such a fancy piano," I say.

"If you want to tickle the ivories, play away." She sits next to me, hits a few chords, and music bounces around the room. "How about I show you a duet? Something easy we could do together."

"No, thank you."

"Why, sure you can!" She plays more fast notes, then looks at me. "After my classes? Maybe next week after school?

School's just down the street," she says. "If you're planning to be here awhile."

I'm not sure how to answer. When my grandparents couldn't take care of me anymore, my uncle rode a bus from Alaska to Kentucky to get me. But he wasn't about to stay there. Claimed there's nothing back at the farm for him, never was. So he took me from the school where I'd been in the same class with the same twelve kids forever. Here in Destiny, I'll be the new kid for the first time in my life, and the school year's about ended. But that's gotta be better than sitting upstairs tossing a baseball up and down by myself, right?

"Yessum. I'll start school Monday." I glance down at my balled-up fists, then back at Miss Sister. "But I don't know about the piano. My uncle said not to play."

"Why on God's green earth not?" she says. "That's just plain silly."

"I don't think he appreciates my music. Hate to make him mad." *Mad enough to up and leave me at some foster home and never come back* is what I don't say.

"A fine, polite boy like you make anybody mad? I bet that's just not possible." She pats my hand and smiles. "No music? Humph. Over my dead body."

Extra chores. Make up the beds tight with that military

fold thing Uncle Raymond taught me. Keep getting straight As in school. Follow the rules. My head's spinning, but I can do it. When Miss Sister taps across the shiny studio floor and out the door, I begin to play her piano like all ten of my fingers are on fire.

CHAPTER FOUR

The Way to Wash the Laundry

When Miss Sister's Saturday morning students start piling out of their cars, it's time to disappear. No way am I getting caught in the middle of a floor full of giggling girls in their dance outfits.

I race upstairs and grab the list propped on our nightstand.

> FIND OUT WHERE THE LAUNDROMAT'S AT.
> REMEMBER WHITES SEPARATE FROM DARKS.
> HANDKERCHIEFS AND UNDERSHIRTS FOLDED IN SQUARES.

I wad up Uncle Raymond's note and *bing!* — into the corner wastebasket like a strike in a catcher's mitt.

Before I can get out of my room and downstairs with the dirty laundry, tires screech and a car door slams right under my window. I push the curtain to one side, open the window a little. A girl's stepping out of a convertible. Long black ponytail. Bright orange sneakers. Braves baseball cap. She's holding a pair of shiny shoes with her thumb and one finger, her arm stretched way out like they've stepped in something smelly.

"Don't need a ride," she says. "I'm walking home after dance class." The girl shifts her bag across one shoulder and turns toward the Rest Easy.

The lady driving the blue Cadillac leans to look at herself in the side mirror. She straightens her hat and peers over huge sunglasses. "I'll be at my Destiny Day Art in the Park meeting. Enjoy your tap class, Anabel dear," she calls out.

"Bye, Mom" is all the girl says. Then the car tires crunch in the gravel, the convertible pulls away, and that lady doesn't even notice her six-foot-long scarf caught in the door, waving like a flag on the Fourth of July.

Grabbing our laundry, I head downstairs and onto the porch just as the girl tosses her knapsack and shiny shoes into a thick bed of purple flowers. She walks away from the Rest Easy fast. I wonder where she's going. Then I remember where I'm going. The Laundromat.

Inside the studio, Miss Sister's already calling out "Shuffle! And tap! And turn two three!" — warming up her class.

When I step back into the front hall, that kid Mamie sticks out her tongue and rushes past me toward the crowd of girls in pink leotards. Ignoring her, I find a note on the kitchen bulletin board.

MAGIC COIN LAUNDROMAT,
CLEAN AND CONVENIENT
3 AZALEA ROAD, OFF MAIN STREET
TUESDAYS ARE FREE SOAP DAYS

I quickly head to the sidewalk and cross the street. Pretending to be out for a walk in the hot Florida sunshine instead of hauling dirty clothes and detergent to the Magic Coin.

Until the girl in the Braves cap glances back.

Did she see me? The last thing I need is to get caught carrying my uncle's smelly laundry! What if she's in my class on Monday? I should slink away before she notices.

Plan A: Walk as fast as I can. On the opposite side of the sidewalk.

Plan B: Run even faster back to the Rest Easy.

Too late.

The girl's stopped dead still in the middle of the sidewalk. I'm about to run smack-dab into her. Yikes! I can't breathe!

What to do with the dirty underwear? I toss my bag behind a tall blooming bush and leap back on the sidewalk.

"Hey there." She looks straight at me. Whew, she's smiling. Maybe she didn't notice I just zigzagged on and off the sidewalk with a big bag of underwear. "My name's Anabel Johnson. What's yours?" She's almost as tall as I am, but she talks ten times faster.

"Theo Thomas," I manage to squeak out.

"How come I don't know you? I've lived in Destiny all my life. There's only my junior high." She gives me the once-over. "You do go to school, right?"

My huge tongue's stuck in my mouth. I'll never be able to talk to this girl. Why aren't I back home in Kentucky where I know every single kid in my entire school? I swallow and finally answer, "Just moved here. I'll start Monday. Sixth grade."

She looks me over. "Are you smart?"

Huh? I gulp, not sure what to say. "Math's my favorite subject. And history. I guess I'm smart in that."

"Listen up. Mr. Wyatt. Sixth-grade social studies, second period," she says, pushing long black bangs off her forehead and fanning herself. She keeps walking. Since she's still talking, I try to keep up. "He's the good teacher. You'll get him if you're smart. Or if your parents push you into his class like mine did. My daddy's the mayor of Destiny."

Ha. My parents definitely won't be getting me into Anabel's second-period social studies class. They died when I was four. But living on my grandparents' farm — practically forever — I mostly made As.

"Gotta go. See you later. Monday at school, right?" Anabel smiles again and disappears down a side street right near the Magic Coin Laundromat.

Which, unfortunately, is where me and my dirty clothes are headed. I race back to grab the hidden laundry bag.

Inside the steaming-hot Laundromat, a little girl's picking her nose in front of the blaring TV, glancing from Miss Piggy to her mother stuffing the washer with a hundred towels. Trying to ignore the smell of bleach making me gasp for breath, I toss handkerchiefs, white shirts, and Uncle Raymond's dirty socks in a washing machine. Add exactly one cup of Tide Super Clean. Drop a quarter into the slots. For about a second, I dangle my new bandanna over the hot, soapy water. See how Uncle Raymond likes it when his white shirts turn pink. See if my uncle orders *me* to do laundry again. I jerk the red bandanna back. Nope. Not making him mad about shirts. Not since I discovered Miss Sister's piano.

I sit on a washing machine, tapping out a tune. Made-up music's bopping around in my head like my third-grade times tables. *Ba dada dada, yeah!* I can't wait to sneak back to the dance studio.

Then I see her. Anabel! Right near the front window. I hop down and look for a place to hide. Or a way to pretend I belong here. The soda machine! I fumble in my pocket for a dime, push it in, and wait for a cold drink to drop. With my back turned to Anabel Johnson, of course.

Too late. She breezes up. "Hey, you again. Theo. What are you doing here?"

I blab something about got lost, checking out where the Laundromat is 'cause we just moved here, need a grape Nehi. She shrugs like everybody might hang out with their uncle's dirty laundry at the Magic Coin on Saturdays.

Anabel points across the street. "I'm waiting for the movie. The bargain show. Cokes are cheaper here than over at the Clearview." She drops her money in the machine and grabs her drink. "You want my world-famous tour of Destiny before the movie starts?"

When she heads for the door, I stash the Tide inside my laundry bag and follow her.

Anabel nods toward a line of palm trees. "The best thing about this town? The beach. Two streets thataway." She stops under the banner about Destiny and that *Town Time Forgot* thing and shows me a wooden marker right near the post office.

I reach down to touch the letters, avoiding the green pricker plant growing around it. "The yellow paint on the sun's almost rubbed off. Must be old," I say.

"Old and nobody pays attention to it." She touches her baseball cap.

I read the faded marker: *Atlanta Braves Home Away from Home.*

"What? The Braves played here?" I ask.

"Just up the road. Braves spring training. Supposedly, once upon a time, famous baseball players *lived* in Destiny. Daddy says nobody notices the sign, even once Hammerin' Hank started chasing the record." She looks around, then whispers, "I'm thinking of changing that."

Anabel's eyebrows go up in a question, but all I can think about is *Whoa! Hammerin' Hank Aaron?*

I pat the skinny book that's almost always in my back pocket and smile about as big as the sun on that marker. "Home run king. Passed Babe Ruth's record. Henry Aaron's my all-time favorite player ever."

"Cool, Theo!" Anabel ignores my dopey grin and nods like I've won the prize on the *$10,000 Treasure* TV game show. Then she turns toward the movie theater. "Movie's starting soon. See you Monday at school," and she disappears into *The Revenge of the Giant Tarantulas.*

Before we left my grandparents' farm, Uncle Raymond warned me, *Don't set your hopes high. Just means disappointment.* But there are two things I care about. And it's not man-eating spiders and the best detergent for getting out stains.

Number One: Playing Miss Sister's piano.

Number Two: Hank Aaron breaking records.

Yeah, I know. Dream on, Theo. Right? But I can't help it, my hopes are up. Only one day in Destiny, Florida, and already I'm thinking this may be okay.

CHAPTER FIVE

A Boy Needs Rules

By the time I get back to the Rest Easy's front porch, the Saturday morning dance classes are over. Before I can sneak inside the studio, here comes Uncle Raymond dragging up the sidewalk, clanking his heavy tool chest. I race upstairs with our clean laundry. Where that kid Mamie's standing in the hall, boring a hole through me.

"What ya got?" She's doing that hand on her hip thing.

"Nothing," I answer.

"Sure is a big bag of nothing. Lemme see." She grabs for the laundry. I whip it over my shoulder and quickly back into my room. Mamie sticks her tongue out and shuts her door.

Great. Terrorized by a five-year-old.

Hurrying to put away clean laundry before my uncle shows up, I'm smiling about Anabel. Thinking at least one sixth grader in Destiny knows my name. Somebody who likes baseball, same as me. I'll get the good social studies teacher. Have a friend to sit with at lunch on Monday! I'm whistling Miss Sister's music and dreaming about her piano.

Till the door bangs open and Uncle Raymond storms into the room. Pulling off his greasy uniform shirt, he tosses it onto my bed. "Take this. For next Saturday's washing." He looks around the room. "You get your chores attended to? You see my note?"

Before answering, I reach into my shorts pocket to touch the shiny good-luck piece Granddaddy gave me. "Yessir. Read the note. Followed your directions." I concentrate on turning my uncle's white handkerchiefs into perfect squares the way he showed me.

"Don't think you took much time making that bed. You spend a day in the army, you know how to make a bed up." Uncle Raymond's pacing around the room. "Didn't your granddaddy teach you a thing? Sure made me work hard when I was coming up on that blasted farm."

Since my uncle hasn't ever talked about growing up, all I know was he couldn't get away from his family fast enough. "Granddaddy taught me plenty," I say quietly.

"Don't seem like you had rules," he answers. "A boy needs rules."

Under my breath, I curse my uncle's rules.

Grabbing my shoulder, he wheels me around to face him. He shoots me the evil eye and says, "I'm heading out. You hear me? Don't be running all over town getting in trouble, neither. Number one rule, be home before dark."

"I don't have any place to run to," I say, pulling away from him. "Where're you going?"

"Meeting somebody at the diner for supper. Mostly, I keep my business to myself. But this is work." Uncle Raymond opens a drawer, digs through his folded underwear. "Thought you did shirts today, boy."

I hand him a blue shirt.

"Not my work shirt. My dress shirt." When I reach into the laundry bag and pull out a wrinkled — but clean! — white shirt, he says, "Needs ironing." He sniffs the shirt, shakes it out. "You know how to iron?"

"Never learned that one," I mumble.

"No need to get smart." He throws water on his face and slicks back his hair. "Won't be gone long. You better not be sneaking down to that piano. Need your word on that."

I move closer to the tiny closet and pretend to line up pants on hangers. "Not playing the piano." If I'm not looking at my uncle, telling a lie doesn't count. I turn around and nod. But a nod's not my word.

Uncle Raymond sprays a shot of Ban extra-duty deodorant

under both arms, tucks the wrinkled shirt into his pants, and frowns at the mirror. "Hang my shirts on one side, pants on the other." Opening the door, he turns back. "One more thing. If we stay together, you need to learn how to iron," he says, then he's down the stairs, fast.

"If we stay together? Is that what you said? Where would I go?" I follow him into the hall. But he doesn't look back. I stomp back into our room, muttering, "Sure thing, Uncle Raymond. I'll learn how to iron right after you learn how to thank me for ironing." I cram his underwear in the drawer and head downstairs.

When I pass her room, Mamie's door shuts softly. This time, I don't hear a peep out of that brat.

On the back of the Rest Easy Rooming House, somebody's hammered a screen up and turned half the porch into a store-room. Faded beach towels, two fishing poles, about a million flip-flops — not necessarily matched up with a partner — pile up in a big basket marked *Lost and Found*. I dig out a chair with one leg wobbling and the seat half busted and pull it near an open window.

Inside the studio, a blur of pink fabric flits across the window. I lean in closer. Miss Sister! She's humming and there's a tapping sound. Then, *bam!* My chair and my rear end hit the porch floor. Next thing I know, Miss Sister's standing over me, shaking her head.

"Oh my stars, Theo. Are you back here stirring up a racket? Get up and sit with me a while. Scoot over, Ginger," she says to a shaggy dog spread out on the top step. Ginger glares, next thing to a growl. Once she's shooed her dog off, Miss Sister pats the top step next to her and I sink down. "Ginger Rogers is ancient, going on fifteen," she says. "All she's good for is chasing little lizards. I love her just the same."

Now Ginger has taken over the shadiest spot at the bottom of the steps. I scoot down to pet her. She shows me her sharp little teeth.

"She doesn't take to new people. Just ignore her." Miss Sister pulls out a hankie and fans herself. "Anybody with a grain of sense stays out of the sun. But this big oak tree makes my back porch about the coolest place late in the afternoon."

I lean over to grab a handful of dried-up grass shriveling near the bottom step. "I'm not used to Florida," I say. "Never been anyplace so hot."

"Your uncle wrote about a room. Happy to have a vacancy." She points to the little sign in the back window.

"Where all have you fellows lived, Theo?"

"My uncle had a good job up in Alaska." Which he tells me about once a day, but I don't say that. "Me, I lived with my grandparents on their farm. Till they got sick." I bite my lip, remembering what Uncle Raymond warned me about keeping family business to myself.

"Well, you're here now. I hope you'll stay awhile." Miss Sister stands up and tucks a red curl behind her ear. "You want to come inside and play my piano? Unless you have something better to do. Like your laundry?" She raises an eyebrow that makes me wonder what she thinks about Uncle Raymond's rules.

When Miss Sister wiggles an armful of jangly bracelets my way, I push that *if we stay together* thing my uncle said out of my head. She does a dance step, hands on her hips, kicking and swinging all the way to the piano. Of course, I follow her.

Wow! Miss Sister can play and talk at the same time and doesn't miss a beat. "In case you hadn't noticed, our town is about to celebrate Destiny Day. Folks dress up as old-timers from the 1800s when we were founded. June 1874! Exactly one hundred years ago next month!" Her fingers run up and down the keyboard. "I'm staging a special dance recital. 'Boogie Woogie Bugle Boy' is a favorite! It's kind of complicated. But the Mexican hat dance and 'Glow Worm' songs?" She flaps her hand to show how simple it will be, then plays a few chords of the hat dance thing. "You want to try?" she asks, and she slides over to one side of the bench.

I move the sheet music over and peer inside. When I hit a note, those soft things jump up like they're saying hello. I touch a black key, quietly at first, then a white one. So what am I worrying about? Uncle Raymond's long gone. My fingers fly up and down the keyboard. Again, then again. Faster! I finish my made-up song, with a few hat dance notes thrown in. Then I sit back and touch a tiny ray of sunlight jumping off the shiny finish.

She sighs, then asks, "Who taught you, Theo?"

"Taught myself. My grandparents told me Mama first showed me piano notes. But my parents were killed in a car crash when I was little."

"I'm sorry to hear that." Miss Sister squeezes my hand.

"It's okay. I don't really know much about my parents. Except that Mama was a musician. Daddy, too."

I look at my hands resting on the smooth keys, wondering whose long piano fingers I inherited. For sure, my eyes came from my daddy. Maybe that's why Uncle Raymond doesn't like looking me straight in the eye. I heard him and Granddaddy arguing about Daddy the day Uncle Raymond showed up at the farm to claim me.

Pushing that picture out of my head, I shut my eyes and quiet music pours onto the keyboard. Even if it doesn't make me forget my uncle completely, playing this piano takes me someplace else.

When I stop, Miss Sister puts her tiny hand on top of mine. "Theo, that music's a dream," she says.

"I've only played on our old piano at the farm. School didn't have music classes."

"Good music is all about the harmony. You know harmony?" Miss Sister stretches her hand into a chord and I play the same notes, only lower.

"Nice. Harmony." Soon I'm playing the Mexican hat dance better than she does.

"Does the music just hop out of your head, honey?" Miss Sister asks.

"No, ma'am. It jumps out of my fingers." I laugh and play faster now, humming, pumping the shiny pedals.

When I stop, Miss Sister says, "Once your uncle hears you, he'll be downright busting with pride."

"I'm not sharing a single thing with Uncle Raymond. He won't want me being at the piano with you."

"We'll see about that," she says. I play until the sun sneaks low out the front window. Finally, Miss Sister sighs and says, "I should help Mrs. Hernandez with supper. You sit here a while longer, honey."

She doesn't move yet, so I play another jazzy tune from the radio in our room. Then a song I heard in Spanish coming from another radio early this morning. The words and melodies jumble around in my head, coming out perfectly together on Miss Sister's piano.

Her hands go right up to the frilly collar covering her heart and she says, "Truly, Theo, you have a God-given talent."

Over the music I say, mostly to myself, "We're gonna have to figure out a way to break *that* news to my uncle."

CHAPTER SIX

Sunday at the Rest Easy

Miss Sister's Rules for Sundays

No checkers or card playing till after 1:00.

Serve yourself. Peanut butter and bread are on the tables.

Rinse your dirty plates and leave them in the sink.

I dance like nobody's business all week, but Sundays are my quiet days.

S. Grandersole

On our first Sunday at the Rest Easy, I read Miss Sister's note tacked up in the dining room, then grab my baseball glove and head outside. As far as I can tell, there's no rule against thumping a fuzzy tennis ball against the toolshed extra hard. Even on Sundays.

Thwack! Slam the ball, catch it on a bounce. Again.

Again. Till I hear a voice across the tall hedge, coming from the alley.

"Psst. Theo? That you?"

I stop thwacking and turn. Anabel! Sneaking around the bushes, also holding a glove. And a baseball.

She leans around me to look toward the back door of the Rest Easy. "What are you doing here? Where's Miss Sister?"

"Don't know where Miss Sister is right now, but I live here."

"Huh?" Anabel backs away. "You live here? With Miss Sister?"

"With my uncle." There. I said it. Maybe she won't mind being friends with the new kid who lives at the Rest Easy Rooming House with his uncle who forces him to make up his bed with some stupid military fold thing and do the laundry every Saturday.

Fat chance.

For now, she keeps talking, taking big steps backward toward the shed. "I was on my way to the school. Looking for somebody to catch with. Didn't know you played," Anabel says, and she tosses me a hard, low ball, overhanded.

"I was a pretty good shortstop, before." I drop my tennis ball and field her grounder.

"Before you moved here? Too bad you didn't get to Destiny before they picked summer teams."

Yeah, well, no way my uncle cares about signing me up for something I really might love.

Anabel stands up straight and looks right at me. "Hey, maybe they'll bend the rules. We don't get new players who are any good." She punches her mitt and waits for my throw. "I bet it's no fun. Being new."

"Doesn't matter one way or the other." I toss the ball up and down and kick at the dirt to show her I don't care. I throw her a high ball just as my uncle appears on the back steps. I glance over. He nods. I ignore him.

"That man's looking for you." Anabel holds her baseball up, asking if I'm ready.

"He can wait."

When she hears Miss Sister rattling around in the kitchen, Anabel turns around quick and slips through the back hedge. "Gotta go. Can't let her catch me."

"Wait a minute! What's the big deal?" But she's raced off down the alley and I'm inside the dining room without finding out why she's avoiding Miss Sister.

Even this Sunday lunch is a whole lot tastier than what my uncle fixed the week we waited to leave Kentucky. He didn't learn how to cook from my grandmother, that's for sure. We pile potato chips on top of our sandwiches and grab a couple of homemade brownies. Except for two old men arguing about whether it's about to rain, the dining room's empty. We sit at one end of the long table.

"Who was that out back?" Uncle Raymond takes a big drink of his sweet tea.

"Just a girl. In sixth grade. I'll probably see her at school tomorrow. Maybe we'll be friends."

"Maybe," my uncle grunts. He finishes his sandwich, tightens the top to the pickle jar, and stands up.

"Definitely we'll be friends," I say even though I have no clue.

Uncle Raymond sits back down. "It don't pay to get attached to people. Even to a place." He narrows his eyes at the old men at the end of the table swapping fish stories.

"I like it here," I say.

"Don't matter what you like. I'm not sure about this here place, Destiny. Tire changing's beneath me. Learned engine repair in the army." Uncle Raymond wads his paper napkin up by his plate just as Miss Sister sashays over to our table.

"Good afternoon, boys. Enjoying those brownies?" she asks.

My uncle barely looks up.

"Yes, ma'am." I stand up and answer. Miss Sister smiles and I think that's a wink. I smile back like we're sharing a secret.

"Made them myself. We usually don't fix Sunday meals; Mrs. Hernandez's day off. But you being new and all." She gives my shoulder a squeeze. "Just wanted to make you welcome. You need anything, let me know."

When she moves toward the kitchen, my uncle glowers. "Don't need people getting in my business," he mutters, and I worry whether he means Miss Sister or me.

I push my chair in and walk toward the kitchen, balancing my plate and glass. Uncle Raymond follows. He stands close to me, scraping leftover potato chips into the trash.

"Where're you off to in such a hurry?" he says.

"Nowhere." I need to get away from my uncle so I can breathe better. Before he can grab me, I say, "Back later," and hurry toward the door.

Just off the front porch, a tall white bird creeps closer to the brightest red flowers I've ever seen. Slipping out the front door, I walk fast toward the sound of squawking seagulls, remembering what Anabel said is the best thing about Destiny. I glance over my shoulder every third step, jogging down the sidewalk. Pretty soon, I see the pier. At the end of the dock, a pelican perches on a bucket of fish guts, staring at me. Two guys throw fishing lines into the water. Off in the distance, a sailboat catches the wind and speeds up.

"Wow, cool!" Yikes. Did I just say that out loud? Yep. I love it here, though. Sinking down onto the beach, I lean against the seawall. A smell I don't know — warm sunshine and salt water mixed together — makes me think I could stay in this town forever. I let the sand sift through my fingers and picture me — maybe with Uncle Raymond — out there fishing. I'm daydreaming about catching the biggest fish in the universe when a shadow blocks the sun.

"What you doing? Ain't you got something better to do?"

I'd recognize that snarl anywhere.

Uncle Raymond's work boots kick at the sand. His arms are crossed. Miss Sister's little dog's behind him, also snarling.

I jump up to face him eye to eye. And to get away from Ginger Rogers. "Sure is nice at the ocean," I say.

"Told you once already. Not the ocean. Gulf of Mexico." Uncle Raymond jabs a finger at my chest, hard. "Waste of time, the beach. You've seen enough," he says, then turns and heads back toward the sidewalk.

"We could fish," I call out. "That's not wasting time. Granddaddy and I used to catch trout in the farm pond."

He stops and waits till I catch up with him. "I fished all the time in Alaska. Before I had to leave so quick." Uncle Raymond stares out at the water. "No time for that now."

When Miss Sister's dog looks up at him and wags her tail, I say, "Ginger Rogers followed you? Miss Sister says she doesn't take to strangers. Sure doesn't like me."

Uncle Raymond lets the little dog lick his hand. "All animals take to me. Your mama and I had a goat. Named him Charlie. Chewed up one of your mama's doll babies. Made her mad as the dickens."

Whoa! That's as much as my uncle's ever said about my mama. I hold my breath, waiting for more. Instead, Uncle Raymond scratches the dog's ears, then walks away from me. "Git on back to your room," he hollers over the sounds of the ocean.

Make that *the gulf*.

As soon as we open the screen door, Miss Sister calls out from the front room, "Wipe the sand off your feet, boys!" She's leaning over, turning the knob on the TV to one of those movies where dancers make big circles and kick to old-timey music. My grandmother loved those old movies.

Uncle Raymond drags his heavy boots across her red-and-pink doormat, then starts toward the stairs, but I say hello to Miss Sister before following him.

"Come sit with me! Bet there's a baseball game on here somewhere. Don't mind changing the channel one bit. I'll get us some iced tea." She jumps up and flounces off before Uncle

Raymond can escape upstairs. I tune the TV, then collapse onto the sofa. Sitting on a straight-backed chair as far away from me as he can get, my uncle crosses his arms and glares.

When Miss Sister hands me my tea, I say, "Braves game today. Hank Aaron already passed Babe Ruth's record. Now everything's gravy."

She passes around her brownies. "Here you go, boys. Now let's see who can hit one out of the park."

"If anybody can, Hank Aaron can," Uncle Raymond says. Then he jumps, kind of like he's surprised himself, talking to Miss Sister about baseball. He doesn't say another word until the game ends. "Thanks for the tea," he mumbles, and stomps up the stairs without even a look back. Miss Sister raises her eyebrows, but we don't talk, just sit together drinking our iced tea. The last place I want to be is upstairs with my uncle. The first place I want to be is here. Near Miss Sister, not too far from her piano.

CHAPTER SEVEN

Theo the Bumblebee

On Monday morning, my stomach thinks I've eaten chicken and gravy for breakfast when all I've done is gulp down a glass of water at the bedroom sink.

Grabbing the big brown envelope from my top drawer, I don't look at Granddaddy's picture postcards that still keep coming. Instead, I take out my school records and race toward the front door. Where I almost run into Miss Sister wearing a dress that looks like she's stolen somebody's orange-flowered curtains.

"Barely seven o'clock and already too hot to move." She stops dancing around her broom, sweeping up that slithery Spanish moss stuff that hangs off most every tree in Destiny. "Oh my lands, your first day of school! Do you have all the paperwork?" Miss Sister peers around me. "Where's your uncle?"

"Uncle Raymond can't miss work. Early shift. He called ahead, told them I was coming." I hold up my birth certificate and my report cards from Kentucky. Starting school this close to summer vacation may not be the smartest move, but it's better than being stuck upstairs in my room. Alone. Friendless.

Miss Sister squints at my report cards flashing in front of her face. For a minute I think she's about to ask another question, but she pats me on the shoulder and shoos me down the sidewalk. "Principal Jackson's little girl is one of my dancers. You need anything, he'll take good care of you." She points down the street. "One block down, then turn left. James Weldon Johnson Junior High School's written across the building. You can't miss it."

I crunch across a neighbor's driveway made of shells bleached so white I shield my eyes. Great. First day at school and already my loser-new-kid T-shirt's a dripping ball of sweat. When I push open the heavy front door, a blast of frigid air-conditioning hits me.

In the middle of the wide hall, I stop dead still. A million framed pictures stare out. Classes of kids who've probably known each other since they left baby teeth under their tooth fairy pillows. Or banged up their knees falling off monkey bars in kindergarten. Like me and the friends I left back home. I may never ever be a part of Destiny, Florida, but I trudge off to find the principal's office, eyes straight ahead, avoiding looking at the walls of Johnson Junior High.

I'm praying I don't run into Anabel while I'm holding my school records for the whole world to see: *Thelonious Monk Thomas*. What did I do to deserve a name that hard to pronounce and easy to make fun of? What were my parents thinking?

When I finally pass Anabel, she's surrounded by girls in softball shirts and she's racing so fast down the hall, she doesn't even smile. Dream on, Theo. Just because she bothered to ask my name and toss around a baseball with me doesn't mean we're friends.

By the time I figure out where my classrooms are, not to mention my locker combination — 9L-8R-3L-6R — it's sixth-grade lunch. I inch my way through the cafeteria line. Hot dogs floating in slimy water. Canned peaches that have probably been there since last week. I grab a grilled cheese and a carton of milk and survey the crowd.

Is every lunch period in every junior high in the world the same? Groups huddled together with their backs turned to anybody different? My T-shirt is neon yellow and black. I look like a tall bumblebee. Uncle Raymond cut my hair way too short. No way I'm sitting with the boys wearing those patrol belt things. Not the jocks lobbing rolls across their table, either. I add an apple and cookie to my orange plastic tray and slide into a corner table to read my milk carton and wish I was back in Kentucky.

"Hey, Theo." Anabel! She waves a carrot stick from two tables over. "Remember me?"

Of course I remember the only sixth grader who's said a single word to me in my entire lifetime in Destiny.

"Wanna sit here?" She pats the metal chair next to her. A boy stops eating to hang on her every word. She glares at him and at a girl rolling her eyes at my bumblebee shirt. I settle on the empty chair and bite into my grilled cheese. Cold and hard.

"Everybody around here a Braves fan?" I ask, reading her T-shirt.

"Not everybody. Me, though. Your team's the Braves, right?" Anabel stops polishing her apple to wait for my answer.

"Yep." I twirl the straw in my lukewarm milk and wonder how it would feel to hang out with Anabel and her friends, talk about baseball. Maybe I'll start by offering her the oatmeal cookie on my tray. I glance down at her lunch. Carrots, the apple, chips, a chocolate cupcake with squiggles on top. A thermos with her name on it. I stuff my boring brown cookie in my mouth.

Anabel points a potato chip at me. "Remember what I told you about the Braves and spring training?"

"You mean that sign downtown?"

"There's more baseball in Destiny than that marker near the post office." She raises her eyebrows and says, "Daddy says a lot of players lived around here. My mom says 'Who cares?'"

"Your mom's not a fan?" I fiddle with my grilled cheese.

"She's a fan of girls learning to dance," Anabel says. "Ridiculous, huh?"

Before I can answer, a deafening buzzer signals the end of lunch, so loud I almost choke on my sandwich. After that, chairs start clanging and scraping, kids laughing and talking. "Later," Anabel mouths and follows the crowd. I dump my tray and head for the cafeteria door.

By last-period math, a substitute teacher and the window air conditioner sound like they are about to give out. I'm scribbling musical notes across the top of my homework assignment, trying to stay awake. Anabel's three seats in front of me, close enough so I can read the buttons pinned to her knapsack: *Eat Your Veggies, Make Friends Not War, Softball Rocks.* I'm daydreaming about playing a jazzy piano tune for her. Catching a spring training game together next season. Surfing at the beach.

"Hey, psst, you. Theo."

Huh? Who knows my name?

The boy in front of me passes something behind his back. *Theo Thomas* is written in curly script across a tightly folded square of paper. I look around, checking the faces, then slip the note in my shorts pocket. When the bell finally rings, I dart out the door.

Shielding my eyes from the sun that bounces off the black-top, I walk fast, patting my pocket about fifteen times. Yep, still there. I turn the corner, head for the Rest Easy's front porch, and sink onto the front steps. I unfold the note and read:

Dear Theo,
Meet me near the beach at Dawson's Bait Shop.
Tomorrow, 3:30 sharp.
Don't be late!
Your friend, Anabel

Wow, Anabel! My *friend* Anabel wants to go fishing? Maybe walk over to the beach? But my uncle's ordered me to do homework first, every day after school, no matter what. Not to mention, he isn't too crazy about wasting time. If

Uncle Raymond thinks the piano is a waste of time, for sure he'll think kicking back on a beach chair is.

My head's spinning!

Tomorrow, right after school, if I can find Dawson's Bait Shop, I'll be there.

CHAPTER EIGHT

Wishes and Bait Crickets

On Tuesday after school, Anabel's waiting under a sign:

Night Crawlers 50¢ a Bucket.

"Did you get lost?" she asks, tapping her watch.

"Geez. I'm not that late." I'm not telling her it took me at least fifteen minutes to come up with a lie for my uncle about breaking his Homework After School, No Exceptions rule. Yeah, I know. I should be sitting at the Rest Easy writing my essay about "What I Will Do This Summer." I'd rather be at Dawson's Bait Shop with Anabel. "Had to stop by the Rest Easy first," I tell her.

"Hey. You know Miss Sister, right?" Anabel asks.

"Remember, I live at her rooming house."

"You wouldn't tell her about me skipping dance class last Saturday?"

"You skipped?" I smile. "I thought you tossed those tap shoes into the petunias to make them smell better."

"Very funny, Theo." She starts toward the bait shop, then stops. "You don't actually *like* listening to that tap-dancing music all day long, do you?"

Actually, yes. I love the music. Some days Miss Sister's piano reminds me of my life at my grandparents' farm. And even before that, of somebody who showed me middle C when I was barely big enough to reach the keyboard.

Instead of confessing, I say, "What's up with you and dance classes?"

She sinks onto the wooden bench in front of Mr. Dawson's shop. "Dancing's as much fun as having a sprained finger, missing the end of softball season last year."

I take a deep breath of salty air and bait shrimp. "Why don't you just quit?"

"My mom loved ballet when she was a kid. She's sure it'll make me graceful." Anabel kicks hard at a wooden crate leaned up against the steps. "What do I care about being graceful? But you know, *moms.*" Rolling her eyes, she drags out the word, then says it again. "Moms. Ugh."

Actually, I don't know. Not really. But maybe I'd have a mom who cared that much about making me good at music, or at anything. She'd be just like Miss Sister, reminding me to practice, playing duets, baking brownies. Hey, I believe in happy endings! Sometimes.

Anabel stands up. "I'm figuring out how to skip the big recital and never take a dancing class again, forever. When Miss Sister's not looking, I sneak out. Go to a movie. Maybe hide from my mom and read a book at the beach."

"We going to the beach?" I ask hopefully.

"Maybe later." She leans over and paws through her knapsack. "You heard about Destiny Day coming up?"

"Miss Sister said something about her recital and a big celebration."

Anabel rolls her eyes like I'm totally out of it. Which I pretty much am. "Forget that recital! Destiny Day takes over the town square. This year people will wear costumes from the olden days. Kind of weird, actually." She holds up a sheet of paper and drops it into my hand. "Behold, Mr. Wyatt's One Hundred Years of Destiny extra-credit project!"

I glance at the notes she's scribbled on the handout. "What's this got to do with me? I only just got here. You think he'll give me extra credit?"

"Listen up, Theo. *I* need a whole lot of extra credit," she says, smiling.

I read the assignment, slowly this time.

Get to know Destiny!

Research an aspect of our town's history (1874-1974).

Present it at the special Destiny Day festival.

File a carefully written and researched document with the
president of the Historical Society.

Anabel points to the paper. "I'm going to find out everything about baseball in Destiny. When and where. And of
course, who. Throw in something that sounds good for more
extra credit, batting averages and home runs. Take a bunch of
pictures. Oh, I don't know. I'm better at the writing part, but
I stink at history. Actually, I stink at math, too. I need help."
She looks right at me. "You."

"Me?" I squeak. Yeah, right. What if I mess this up? Then
instead of having one friend, I'll have zero. I'm real good at
figuring *that* math out.

"You'll be great," she says. "You're smart. You love baseball. It'll be fun."

When I start breathing again, my heartbeat slows down. "I
know a lot about baseball players. There's this book my
granddaddy bought me. When I was about six. Been reading
it ever since!" Geez. That was a dorky thing to admit to.

"Books. Good. Make our research even better," Anabel says.

Okay. Seems easy enough. I can do this!

"I'm in," I say.

"Listen up. I'll explain as we go." She gives two men leaving the bait shop with their fishing rods the once-over and lowers her voice. "For now, this stays between you and me. If my mom gets wind of me doing a baseball project for everybody in town to see, she'll make us put tap shoes on the players."

Picturing Hank Aaron and his teammates tap-dancing, I laugh out loud.

"Be serious!" Anabel steps up to the screen door. "Come on. We need to interview old-timers. Like Mr. Dawson, inside. I already talked to my dad. Got lots of notes."

"Miss Sister's lived here forever. Did you ask her?"

"Theo, get with the program. I'm avoiding Miss Sister. You can interview her." She laughs and says, "Maybe you can help sneak me out of her dance class."

"I'll help with the baseball part," I answer.

Anabel holds up her notebook and pen. "Mr. Dawson's older than anything. He'll know something." She pushes open the door, leaving me on the steps with the assignment sheet. I follow her into Dawson's Bait Shop.

Inside, a man behind the glass case puts down the fish he's cleaning and wipes his hands on his bloody apron. He steps in front of the counter. "Hey there, Anabel. Going fishing?

Got some crickets, penny apiece." He winks. "Special fancy ones, just for you." He's one of those old guys who laughs at his own jokes.

"No fishing today." Anabel opens her notebook to a clean page. She nods my way. "My friend Theo just moved to Destiny. We're doing a school project."

"So what can I do you for, kiddos?"

I stare at the gray beard that reaches to Mr. Dawson's collar and moves up and down when he talks. I wonder if one of those crickets he's selling might be hiding in that bushy beard.

"We're researching the old days of baseball. Daddy claims you know everything," Anabel says.

"I know the younger spring training players came to Destiny. Cheaper than living over in Tampa or St. Pete. 'Bout twenty years ago, let's see, back in the 1950s. Year Ike won the presidency, how I remember it. But my memory's fuzzy."

Anabel's scribbling notes as fast as he's talking, and I'm watching over her shoulder, thinking how I'll never be able to read her chicken scratch. "Ever talk to any of them?" she asks.

"I used to see them over someplace near Gulf Shores Avenue playing catch. Every once in a while, one of 'em would stop by my place for shrimp or crickets." Mr. Dawson has what my grandmother called smiling eyes. If a person's eyes were smiling, you could trust them for sure, she always said.

"You remember any of the players' names?" I ask, stepping up next to Anabel.

"I remember a tall, skinny guy in particular."

"Who's that?" Anabel stops drawing what I guess is a map of Destiny and looks up.

"That Hank Aaron fellow. Just passed Babe Ruth's record."

I knew it! Fate! I've ended up in Destiny. The same as Hank! Smiling like nobody's business, I bite my lip to keep from blabbing about seeing him play one time, telling everything I know about Hammerin' Hank.

"Nobody paid much attention back then," Mr. Dawson says. "Nice young man, near as I remember."

Before the words escape from my mouth, wondering how anybody could forget anything about Hank Aaron living in Destiny, Anabel closes her notebook. Then Mr. Dawson taps his forehead and says, "You youngsters work hard! School's 'bout the most important thing." He points to the faded sign on the counter: *Ice and Advice*, then turns back to gutting fish.

"Thanks, Mr. Dawson." Anabel waves, and we're out the door.

"Wow!" I sit on the wooden bench to take it all in, hoping Anabel hasn't heard my geeky *wow*. My head's spinning! But while I'm dreaming about Hank Aaron standing here holding a bucket of bait shrimp, she's halfway down the sidewalk.

"Great stuff, right? Wanna walk by the beach on the way home?" she calls back.

This day can't get much better. If I had to leave my grandparents' farm, if I'd dreamed of a place to end up? The beach, baseball, and a piano would have been there.

Pretty soon, I hear water noises. Birds squawking!

When we stop in front of a sign — a picture of a weird-looking creature with a pointy, sharp thing sticking out of its body — I read out loud, " 'Shuffle Feet for Stingrays.' Yikes. What's that mean?"

"Shuffle your feet underwater. Stirs up the sand. Scares the stingrays off." She moves her feet back and forth, real fast. I try it and land on my rear end.

I jump up, look around to be sure nobody saw that, then stare out at the clear blue water. "Let's get closer," I say.

When we're standing near enough to the water that the wind makes it hard to hear, Anabel asks, "You ever been surfing, Theo?"

"Only been to the beach once," I answer.

And my uncle made me leave as quick as I got here.

"Not a lot of big waves in the gulf unless there's a storm coming," Anabel says. "But I bet you'd be great at surfing."

Except I don't know which end of a surfboard to hang on

to. And my uncle's already threatening to find a new job, probably someplace far away from crashing waves.

"I've barely put my big toe in salt water," I say. "But man, can I swim. Mostly in the creek near my granddaddy's farm."

"This summer, I'll teach you to body surf." Anabel points out to some guys in wet suits, some with boards, some just floating around.

Now we're close enough to the gulf to splash each other. Keeping a watch out for stingrays, I kick off my sneakers to practice that shuffle thing in the water.

"Maybe I'll try surfing," I say. At the beach this summer with Anabel. Cool.

Then I push back one long shirtsleeve and touch the ugly scar running down my arm, almost to my hand. I remember the last wish I made. Sitting in the backseat of my parents' old car. I was barely four years old, telling knock-knock jokes. I'd wished for mint chocolate chip ice cream, hot fudge sauce thick as mud. Mom sang that silly song "I Scream, You Scream, We All Scream for Ice Cream." The next thing was white sheets on a hospital bed. After that, I stopped wishing.

"Earth to Theo?" Anabel punches my shoulder. "What are you thinking about?"

"Nothing much. Just ice cream." That was so long ago, my scar's almost faded. Now I can remember that song and kind of smile.

"Good start to our Destiny Day project, huh? I gotta get home, though. Tonight's family togetherness time in front of *Happy Days* on TV." Anabel hurries past the row of palm trees growing beside the sandy walkway.

Shielding my eyes from the blazing hot sun, I watch the waves pick up and the pelicans dive for fish far out in the water. Truthfully, wishes *are* piling up. To find out about Henry Aaron and the baseball players with Anabel. To push Uncle Raymond so far out of my head, the music takes over. To stay in Destiny, playing Miss Sister's piano forever.

CHAPTER NINE

The 100-Year-Old Banyan Tree and Other Fun Facts

On my third day at Johnson Junior High, by the time I relocate my social studies classroom, the only desk left is so small, that skinny kid Mamie could barely fit in it. While I squeeze myself into the seat, Mr. Wyatt's explaining the Fountain of Youth. Telling us Seminoles lived right near Destiny. He's drawing chalk pictures and rambling on about a hundred-year-old banyan tree still standing in front of the county library. "Page forty-three of your Florida history book. It's famous! A famous tree!"

Mr. Wyatt's a whole lot more excited about the life of that banyan tree than Uncle Raymond is about our life together. Maybe if I ace this project, my uncle'll decide Destiny is A-OK. Big maybe.

Anabel's in the front row, writing as fast as Mr. Wyatt scribbles words on the chalkboard. Other kids raise their hands to nail down their topics, calling out "Seminoles!" and "Old tree!" They consult with partners and review note cards together. I'm still trying to find my pencil.

Before I even open my book, Mr. Wyatt strolls to the back of the room and says — not so loud that everybody's listening — "Theo, maybe you want to participate in our special history project? Learn a little who, what, where, when, how about your hometown?"

"Okay," I answer, turning *hometown* around in my head. I glance at Anabel, thinking she'll chime in.

Mr. Wyatt looks around the classroom. "Care to pick a partner?"

I'm not too great at speaking up in a class I've been a part of for exactly three days. But I sit up straighter, clear my throat, and announce, maybe a little too loud, "Anabel. I'll help Anabel."

Heads pop around. Girls giggle. Guys shake their heads in total disbelief. Pretty much everybody rolls their eyes at the new kid who volunteered to *help* Anabel. But she nods and even smiles, and *Theo Thomas* gets printed on the chalkboard next to *Anabel Johnson*.

"Do you have an idea for your project?" Mr. Wyatt asks, waving the chalk next to our names.

Before I can blurt "Baseball!" Anabel calls out, "We're still working on it, Mr. Wyatt. A few details to figure out."

Okay. Maybe a *few* details. Like that who, what, when thing. Or whether her mom's turning it into a Baseball Players *Dance* in Destiny project.

"Remember" — Mr. Wyatt looks around at his students — "Destiny Day's less than three weeks away. Your reports will go to the Historical Society's files. Saved in perpetuity. If you don't know that word, look it up. Make your projects interesting! Make them fun!" Hands shoot up again. Construction paper's flying. Everybody's going for extra credit in social studies.

I haven't even collected my books or my thoughts before the buzzer blasts the class into next period. Mr. Wyatt makes sure we get our assignment sheets, pick up the markers, and leave his room organized for the eighth-grade world history geniuses lining up outside his door.

"Psst, Theo." Anabel steps closer to my desk and whispers, "Remember. Don't say much about our research yet."

"I thought you were all gung ho about Baseball in Destiny," I answer.

"I have to ease into it. Daddy's helping me prepare my mom."

Mrs. Johnson and Uncle Raymond could get along real good. Good at bossing people around. Stuffing my notebooks into my knapsack, I head to gym class, wondering how exactly we are gonna convince Anabel's mom that baseball's bigger than dancing. But Anabel can worry about that. I'm worrying about getting through this day and back to the Rest Easy's piano before my uncle comes home.

I'd forgotten about Wednesdays. Dance classes will arrive any minute. I drop my school stuff in the hall and open the studio door.

Miss Sister's waiting. "Right here." She pats the empty space next to her. "Just enough time for a few notes before the snowflakes appear."

"Snowflakes?" I look out the window. "It's a hundred degrees in the shade."

She laughs. "My littlest dancers, silly."

I slide onto the piano bench.

She pats my back. "Sit up tall, Theo. Let me hear you swing. Hit those notes hard!" she says, straightening her music book and pointing to the black squiggly things on the page.

"You know I can't read those notes. Just give me the melody." I smile and she nods slowly, humming a few bars, singing about glowworms.

I'm about to play along with her song. But first I glance toward the window, hoping neither dancing snowflakes nor my uncle is lurking on the porch. Miss Sister sees my scrunched-up mouth and of course my hands. I'm sitting on my hands. She stops humming.

"I know you're worrying about your uncle. But what that man doesn't know won't hurt him is all I'm saying. With a little practice, I swear you could be playing 'Boogie Woogie Bugle Boy' for my recital."

I gulp. "Your recital?"

"Put those fingers on the keys! Hands curved! Time's wasting!" Miss Sister plays the glowworm song and I follow along.

What if I do get good enough for her dance recital? Maybe at least Uncle Raymond would understand about me and music.

Or he could lock me in my room for the entire summer — heck, for my entire life — just for disobeying his order: No Piano Playing Ever. Anywhere, Anytime.

CHAPTER TEN

The Problem

At exactly 3:45 the next day, it's a perfect beach day. But I'm trudging up to my room where Uncle Raymond will be waiting. I'm obeying his Homework After School, No Exceptions rule. Baseball project, maybe hang out with Anabel? No way. Not today.

When I open the door, a magazine's in front of his face. It's easy to see the picture on the cover. Snow, lots of snow. And I don't mean Miss Sister's snowflakes, her littlest dancers. Nope. The real thing.

He barely nods. "You go to school today?" he finally asks.

Now, that's about the world's dumbest question. I answer it anyhow. "I went to school."

It might be nice to tell him about the baseball project. It would be nicer to tell him I've been playing the piano, that Miss Sister thinks I'm good enough to play for her dance recital. But he'd just yell. Besides, no way am I talking to somebody not interested enough to put down a magazine.

Uncle Raymond turns the pages, staring at each picture, and yep, the magazine's about his favorite place in the world. Where he ran off to after he got out of the army. A state so much prettier and nicer and cooler and better than Kentucky or Florida or anywhere else he can think of. Except no way can he live in a little cabin in the Alaskan wilderness now. Now he's got me.

I slump down on my bed to open my math homework. Finally, Uncle Raymond stands up and says, "Remember, I got to work late tonight. If you go out, be home before the streetlights come on." He grabs his tool chest, and he's gone.

But he doesn't get far. Miss Sister's at the foot of the stairs. When I hear my uncle's voice drifting quietly from the front hall, I move to the open bedroom door.

"Not your business, ma'am," he's saying. "That's Theo's problem."

Problem? Which problem's that? That I'm never allowed to play the piano as long as I live? That I'm the new kid at school for the first time in my life? That an uncle who hardly knows me wishes I'd never been born?

I creep down the top steps, holding tight to the banister, holding tighter to my breath.

"You listen here, Mr. Raymond," Miss Sister says. "Theo has a special gift. He's learning to express himself through music."

I take two more quick steps down and push my hand into my pocket to touch my good-luck coin.

"That's just your highfalutin way of saying he's been sneaking down to play that piano. I told him to stay away." My uncle's meanness cuts through the upstairs heat and makes me gasp.

Miss Sister's voice changes to a lullaby. "Might as well tell a sparrow not to fly."

"Piano can't lead to nothing good. Messed up his mama for sure."

My knees buckle, but I grab hold of the banister again and stand straight as a stick, still listening.

"Your boy's got a magnificent talent," Miss Sister answers.

"He ain't my boy. And this place never was meant to be permanent. I need to get him away from you and that durn music." Uncle Raymond's voice drops, but I hear every word. "Keeping my options open. Job here ain't good enough. Might have me something new already."

"A new job?" Miss Sister says. "You can't take Theo away from Destiny."

Take me away? Already? I want to run downstairs and holler at Uncle Raymond. I'm not going anywhere! But he's liable to haul off and pop me. For sure, he'll make a new rule about eavesdropping. I wipe my sweaty hands on my jeans, then jam them back in my pockets.

"I can do what I right well please. I'm in charge," my uncle says. "He belongs to me."

"Nobody *belongs* to somebody else. Theo's his own person. He's settling in here. He needs friends and people who love him."

Now my heart's beating so fast, my head's spinning.

"Does your nephew know about this?" Miss Sister speaks louder. "What exactly did you tell Theo?"

"Nothing yet. Not your business. If I get me the new job in Mount Flora, there's a duplex waiting, too. Nice old lady next door offered to watch after him."

"Mount Flora? My stars! Even on the bus, that's over an hour away," Miss Sister says.

"Don't know what difference it makes to anybody 'cept me." Uncle Raymond keeps muttering even while he's shutting the front door, making it hard to hear, harder to believe.

But I know Miss Sister heard every single word. Even the ones he didn't say out loud.

CHAPTER ELEVEN

Money in a Basket

The next day goes by in a big blur of worry. Anabel and I aren't much closer to figuring out our Destiny Day project. Miss Sister's flitting around singing, dancing, and playing the piano by herself. I miss my grandparents and every single thing that happened before Uncle Raymond took me in. And soon we may be moving to someplace called Mount Flora.

By Saturday morning, I'm feeling really sorry for myself. What's worse, it's laundry day.

When I turn back up the street lugging carefully concealed clean clothes from the Magic Coin, Anabel's waiting on the Rest Easy's front porch glider.

I drop the laundry behind a chair and point to her softball cleats. "You plan to dance in those?" I'm trying not to laugh.

"I'm working out a way to skip this dance thing," she says, popping a Peppermint Pattie in her mouth. "Forever. Really, Theo, do I look like a dancer to you?" She pushes the metal glider so hard all those little pillows with sayings sewed on them topple over. Her cleats hit the porch floor, *bang bang bang*, with each push. "My mom's showing up today, so I couldn't exactly cut out and go to a movie. I tried to tell her I have ball practice. But she thinks tap dancing and this recital are way more important than softball drills."

"Maybe you'd like dancing if you tried harder?"

"The only good thing about Miss Sister's class is the jumping part. Might help me with softball." Anabel glares at the dancers prancing up the steps. "Try to convince my mother of that," she says.

Before Anabel punches her Grandersole Dance Academy tote bag to smithereens, her mom's big convertible screeches up. Opening the door, Mrs. Johnson plants her high-heeled shoes firmly on the sidewalk. I shoo a lizard, black as the railing paint he's hiding on, and make myself invisible behind the porch column.

"Hello, Anabel dear. Good morning, dancers. I have notes for you all!" Mrs. Johnson opens her fat briefcase and passes envelopes to girls dressed in pink leotards or wearing black tap shoes. Her eyes pass me once, but I'm a blip on her radar. Gone before it registers.

Anabel glances back and rolls her eyes. "My mom. Beatrice Munez Johnson. Mayor's wife. Former ballet star. Town organizer. She'd like to run this place. Along with everything and everybody else in Destiny," she says under her breath just as Mamie appears.

"Hey, Mrs. Johnson. I'm the star of the 'Glow Worm' song. Mama and me have been saving up nickels in my piggy bank, all for Miss Sister." She puts out her hand, an envelope magically appears, and Mamie bounces into the dance studio.

"What's with the notes?" I ask, moving closer. Mrs. Johnson sure didn't hand *me* a small white sealed envelope with *Theo Thomas* carefully composed in perfect script on the front.

"Money for a gift and flowers for Miss Sister. Everybody gives a few bucks. No big deal," Anabel says.

I sink into the big chair at the end of the porch and tuck my knees up under my chin. "Can you snitch me one?"

Anabel passes me her envelope. "Here. I don't want it."

Calling All Dancers!
We will again be collecting monies for our beloved
Miss Sister Grandersole. This year marks her 15th year

teaching the children of Destiny. We're asking for $5 from each family. Please sign the card and leave your contribution inside the small basket on the front hall radiator.

Mayor Johnson and I have started the ball rolling with our $20 contribution.

Thank you.

Mrs. Beatrice M. Johnson

Sure. Collecting money is as simple as plucking it off the trees and hiding it in a closed-up basket in the Rest Easy's front hall. No big deal.

I crumple the paper and cram the fancy note in my pocket. "That's a lot of money. People really love Miss Sister," I say.

"Every recital, she dances out onto the stage and somebody hands her flowers." Anabel's voice is as cold as a block of ice from the back porch Deepfreeze. "Yep. Everybody loves Miss Sister. I'd love her, too, if she coached softball."

"You still planning to skip out on the recital?" I ask.

"Shhh! My mom doesn't know." She looks toward Mrs. Johnson whispering, smiling at each dancer. "You can't let on to Miss Sister, either."

I swallow hard, worrying about lying to cover for my new friend when she dreams up a fake broken arm or some other excuse to ditch the recital.

"Guess I have to go pretend I'm having fun." Anabel kicks off her cleats and buckles on black tap shoes. "Man, this stinks," she says, tugging at her shorts while clomping off to the studio.

I wait till the kids in their dancing clothes disappear inside and Mrs. Johnson's car speeds off before creeping up the stairs dragging my bag of clean laundry. As my feet hit the carpet, I count each step. One, two, three, four — all the way to twenty. Twenty dollars. More money than I have. Soon to be collecting in a basket on the front hall radiator. My fingers touch Mrs. Johnson's note again, and a big lump settles in my stomach.

I wish I could get something nice for Miss Sister. Too bad I don't have a full piggy bank. Or an uncle willing to fork over money for flowers.

CHAPTER TWELVE

Grooving to Thelonious Monk

For the rest of the afternoon, I forget Mrs. Johnson's money and flowers and white envelopes by memorizing the music drifting up the stairs. After I've tossed a baseball up and down for three hundred repeats of the "Glow Worm" song, the last kid finally packs up her tap shoes. The coast is clear enough. I sneak into the dance studio.

Miss Sister's waiting. "Theo! Your turn now. Come sit with me." She scoots down the piano bench, smiles, and pokes at a curl that's popped out of her rhinestone barrette. The second she taps out a soft tune on the keys, my uncle and his No Piano Playing Ever rule flies out of my head.

"You play the lower chords, Theo. Jazz 'em up!"

"Like that?" I ask, echoing and complicating her notes.

"Like that Thelonious Monk piano man I do believe you're named after," she says over the music.

I stop playing and stare. "Thelonious who?"

"Your namesake. I noticed your official records when you headed off to school on Monday. Just the greatest jazz musician you could imagine." Miss Sister beams. "Your parents knew what they were doing when they gave you *that* fine name."

"I was pretty little when they died. Nobody talked about my name."

"You should be proud of it, honey."

"Once, back in Kentucky, a teacher tried to tell me I was named after somebody famous. My granddaddy said that was a figment of her imagination. Whatever that means. I couldn't hardly pronounce Thelonious then. I pretty nearly forgot what that teacher said."

No matter what's printed on my birth certificate, I'm plain Theo to my grandparents, to everybody now.

"Well, it seems somebody suspected you'd be a musician. You have a natural-born talent. You're living up to your famous name — Thelonious Monk Thomas, pianist." Miss Sister plays a chord, then a few more, swaying to the tune.

When she stops, she turns to a shelf of record albums, flipping aside one after another. "Dance, opera, show tunes. Here it is — jazz!" She pulls out a black vinyl record, holds up the cover. "My favorite! *Monk's Dream.*" She marches right over to her phonograph player and slips it onto the turntable.

Music like I've never heard before drifts across the dance studio. A piano melody sinks all the way to my toes and won't let go. Holding the record cover close, I drum my fingers across his face. Maybe my daddy knew this dude. That's why they named me Thelonious!

Granddaddy always said my mama could have been real famous if she hadn't up and left to marry my daddy. 'Course, he meant famous singing church weddings in Boone County, Kentucky. Not this Thelonious Monk guy that Miss Sister's playing. His music makes my feet jump and my palms pound the piano bench.

When Miss Sister stops swaying to the notes, she lifts the needle off Mr. Monk's record and sits close to me.

"Did my parents want me to play the piano like that?" I ask. "Is that why they named me Thelonious?"

"I suspect that was exactly what they wished for, Theo honey. It's a beautiful name. A gift. You hang on to it."

Before I hand her the album cover, I look one last time at the picture of Thelonious Monk wearing his cool hat, eyes shut, drinking in the music.

All the next day, Thelonious Monk's name and his music and what my uncle said about moving to Mount Flora bounce around my head, fighting for room. When Uncle Raymond finally gets back from his Sunday work shift and tosses his lunch pail down hard on the dresser, I'm still worried. But I'm ready.

He looks at the little clock next to the bed, then back at me. "You awake?"

I'm sitting here in my T-shirt, jeans, and laced-up high-tops. Yeah, I'm awake. But I answer nicely, so as not to make him mad, "It's only eight thirty."

He unbuttons his long shirtsleeves and frowns. "You got school tomorrow. Get to bed," he says.

Still trying my Be Nice thing, I answer, "I've been thinking about baseball. I was a pretty good shortstop back home. I might try to play in Destiny this summer. My friend Anabel thinks maybe they'll let me on her team."

"Ain't smart to make long-term plans." Uncle Raymond turns his back to me and mumbles, "Something might come up."

"What might come up?" When he doesn't answer, I start over. "I heard you and Miss Sister talking. The other night, in the front hall. About leaving."

"You ask too many questions," he answers. "Not your business. Just considering my options."

I slam my math book closed; the Be Nice thing just flew

out the window. "If it's me you're *just considering*, I'm not moving." Standing up fast, I look my uncle straight in the eye. "Especially next door to somebody who's older than dirt."

"You don't know nothing, boy."

"We just got here!" I take a deep, worrying breath and change the subject before I start hollering again. "You ever heard of a piano player named Thelonious Monk? Miss Sister played me one of his records."

He takes a step toward me, chewing on his inside lip, frowning. "That lady needs to mind her own business," he says, his voice a growl.

"He and I got the same name. Maybe Mama and Daddy really liked his music? Maybe even knew him?" The more questions I ask, the tighter my uncle's mouth closes up.

"Never heard of him. Don't know who your mama took up with after she left the farm," he finally says. "Once she went off to that fancy college, met your daddy, she didn't care a thing about me. I was far off, fighting for my country. She was carrying signs, spitting on soldiers. Didn't matter about what our family always stood for. Your daddy and my baby sister, they hated me for doing what's right. The feeling was mutual."

It feels like one of Uncle Raymond's wrenches has jumped out of his tool chest and twisted my heart right out.

"You hated your own sister? For carrying what signs? Why?" My voice is so quiet I don't know whether he's heard me.

My uncle slaps his hand hard on the closet door. *Whap! Whap!* "Don't matter. Shut up about it." He grabs a towel and heads to the bathroom down the hall. "That light better be out before I get back," he hollers over his shoulder.

I'm shaking when I fold my jeans over the straight-backed chair. But I turn out the light just as Uncle Raymond comes back in the room and sits on his bed. "We still here when school's out, you need to figure out something more useful than baseball to do," he says. "And I don't mean playing any durn piano."

I don't bother answering. It wouldn't help. Instead, I squeeze my eyes shut and count to ten, real slow.

Uncle Raymond's boots drop on the floor with a heavy thud. "Whatever happens next, you don't get a say. I gave up a lot to take you in. Good job, more money, all those years working in Alaska."

Like I didn't mind leaving my grandparents, my friends, *my* life. But I'm working to make a song swirl in my head and take over the sound of Uncle Raymond saying, *You don't get a say.* I let my breath out all at once and whisper across the dark room, "We can't leave Destiny. Please."

The only answer is creaking bedsprings, then snoring. Before long, my uncle's yelling about jungles and guns and spit. Under the sheet, I cover my ears and listen for musical beats inside my head. Drumming out the sound of another of his scary nightmares.

CHAPTER THIRTEEN

The Dark and Dusty Attic

After school the next day, I sit on the Rest Easy's front porch glider waiting for Anabel. Pushing away what my uncle said about moving, about my name, and about my parents, I stare at the heat rippling off the street. It's hard not to turn into a sweat ball in Florida.

When Mamie appears and I hustle off down the sidewalk, she follows me. "Hey, Theo," she says between screeched verses of a song about a dog named B-I-N-G-O. "Mama's inside resting. I'm out here being good. Whatcha doing?"

"Nothing." I hear a noise and jump. Fifty green birds are up on the telephone line, squawking so loud they about drown out Mamie's voice.

"Why're you running?" Mamie looks up, then takes another slurp of her red Popsicle. "You scared of parrots?"

"How'd they get here? Parrots live in cages." I shield my eyes from the sun and possible bird droppings.

Mamie puts one hand on her hip and stares like I'm from another world. Which technically I am. "Man, you don't know nothing. Somebody let loose a pet. It kept laying more and more babies. Now they live here. No more cages."

"Birds lay eggs," I say, surveying upward. "Not babies."

She picks at a chigger bite on her knee. "I know that. Everybody knows birds lay eggs. Fish lay eggs, too."

"I wish your parrots would fly off to somebody else's front yard." I look again at those green birds exploding with noise and who knows what else.

Mamie's not shutting up. "Hey, you want to hear a joke? What do sharks love to eat?" She waits for half a second before shouting out, "Peanut butter and jellyfish sandwiches!"

Where *is* Anabel? I glance down the street.

"You looking for Miss Sister? She went to the Winn-Dixie for milk for her coffee and Band-Aids for her bunions." Mamie does a little dance step onto the porch steps and hands me her Popsicle stick with two fingers. Great. Now I'm a human trash can.

"You ever been in her attic? I can try on the costumes from

her attic anytime. Pink and lacy is my favorite," she says. "You can wear the uniforms."

"Uniforms?"

Mamie narrows her eyes. "You wanna play dress-up?"

"Not really."

"Lots of things in Miss Sister's attic." Mamie smiles, sticking a tongue in the empty place where a tooth was, begging to be asked how many she's lost. I don't.

Uncle Raymond warned me about talking too much. When that kid on the bus from Kentucky blabbed at me most of the night, my uncle said ignore him. Don't complain like a baby about leaving my friends and giving away my dog. *Give that boy an inch and he'll take a mile*, so my uncle said. Same with Mamie.

"You coming inside to see my dress-ups?" Mamie hopscotches down the front sidewalk, singing more about the dog named B-I-N-G-O. I press her Popsicle stick into Miss Sister's flowerpot and cover up my ears.

Before I keel over from the heat or boredom from talking to Mamie, Anabel finally shows up. "Where's Miss Sister?" She lowers her voice. "Don't want her to see me. I'm still working on my plan to skip out on the recital."

"She's shopping." Next to the mailbox, Mamie's still singing. When she starts the chorus, we slip away.

"We're going back to Mr. Dawson's. He's gotta remember more," Anabel says. She's walking fast and talking faster, so we're at the bait shop in no time flat.

"Anabel! Glad to see you," he says. "You too, son." He winks and I know he's forgotten my name. He wipes fish blood from his fingers, reaches under the display case, and pulls out a cardboard folder. "Found this for you. If you're still looking for baseball stuff."

We paw through the dustiest, yellowest, oldest collection of newspapers, letters, and who knows what else. Anabel holds up a food-splattered menu from the Chat 'n' Chew — hamburgers for twenty-five cents! — and a photograph falls out.

"Hey, Mr. D? Who are these people wearing baseball caps?" She stares at the faded black-and-white photo, dusts off the faces, and passes it across the counter.

Mr. Dawson holds the picture under his bright light. "Well, Chat 'n' Chew's been there forever, so they could be old baseball players, posed for this picture. Keep it. See what your teacher thinks."

Anabel smiles. You can't help smiling at Mr. Dawson, really. "We'll take it all," she says. "Any more ideas?"

"Let's see." He smoothes out his beard and I step back, thinking about crickets. "How 'bout Miss Sister? Rest Easy's been there awhile, too."

Anabel stops writing in her notebook and looks at me. "Did you hear that?"

"Yep." I nod as she hands me the dusty folder.

Wow. What if a famous player, not a whole lot older than me, maybe even Henry Aaron himself, slept in my very bed? With his glove on the windowsill, same as me. Looking out at stars as big as baseballs, dreaming of homer number 715.

Before we can say "Baseball in Destiny" three times fast, we're outside clutching our treasures and I'm bouncing off the sidewalk.

"Oh man, I knew it! Henry Aaron ate peanut butter at the same table as me." A daydream flits across my brain. Me and Uncle Raymond finding something that proves famous players lived at the Rest Easy. Him helping me, like real parents help their kids. Us standing together at Destiny Day, showing off to the history people. My project preserved in perpetuity! Forever!

I whistle all the way back to the Rest Easy. No sign of Mamie or Miss Sister. Only Mr. Hernandez, outside pushing his lawn mower. Who'll know if I poke around the attic? Mamie claims uniforms are up there. Could they be baseball uniforms? Stranger things have happened! Baseball at the Rest Easy, oh man. Anabel's got her daddy and Mr. Dawson to interview. Her mom might come around and make something fancy for our display. I got nothing.

Hurrying upstairs, I grab my uncle's flashlight. The second door I open leads to the attic steps. I dance light beams on the walls and inch up the dark stairs. Am I about to crunch down on one of those Florida roaches as big as raccoons? Brushing away a spiderweb caught in my hair, my hand bumps something hanging from the ceiling. I jump a mile straight up. Geez Louise, it's just a swinging lightbulb. I pull on the string, and a little circle of brightness sways back and forth. Enough light to see the layer of dust and read labels on boxes stacked high on metal shelves: *Dance Recital, 1959* — and every year after. Moving a stack of 45 records from one shelf to another, I spy a harmonica and blow a few notes, turning them into a soft melody. When I hear a radio start to play downstairs, I stash the harmonica in my pocket and freeze.

What am I doing? Why didn't I ask Miss Sister before coming up here? What if she gets so mad I was messing around in her attic that she won't let me near her piano? What if Uncle Raymond reams me out for sticking my nose where it doesn't belong? Sure, this is my home now. But this feels like trespassing.

I'm about to hotfoot it downstairs with only the old harmonica when I see a gray metal tackle box. Blowing the dust off, I turn it over. Taped on the bottom is a yellowed note card: *Henry left this here.*

Henry?

But the box is locked tight, with a combination. I'll get Uncle Raymond's hammer!

Sure thing. Tools for breaking into something I snatched from the attic of *my* house. Oh man, gotta get out of here. I'll ask Miss Sister and come back later.

What if she says no? Then it's Miss Sister *and* Uncle Raymond mad at me.

But the thing is, if our baseball project turns out, maybe it'll convince Uncle Raymond we need to stay in Destiny.

In no time flat, I'm down the attic stairs with the tackle box hidden under my T-shirt. My heart's pounding! Did Mamie see me? I shut my door softly. I shake the box, banging it against the metal bed frame. Then fiddle with the lock again. No luck.

Stashing the box in our closet behind dirty socks and underwear, I will my heart to slow down. I wash the dust off my hands and hurry downstairs, smiling to beat the band. I totally can't wait to show Anabel tomorrow in school.

Without even turning on the glaring studio lights, I sneak onto the smooth black piano bench and open the keyboard.

When my fingers glide over the keys, my heart's pounding out the beat in time to my thumping bass notes. I change the rhythm to play a tune that's quick, jazzy, bright. Harmony! Music and baseball, Destiny Day with Uncle Raymond! That box from the attic could be the answer to my dreams.

CHAPTER FOURTEEN

Secrets!

*W*hen I come back to our room after supper, my uncle's buttoning up his dress shirt, posing in front of our mirror.

"Where're you going?" I ask.

"Meeting somebody from work. Not much of your business. You learned anything at that new school?" He's good at changing the subject.

I have an idea! I'll tell him about the tackle box in the closet. We'll get his hammer, crack it open, and find baseball treasures!

Or I'll get in big trouble for taking something that isn't mine.

Instead of asking to borrow his hammer, I answer his question. "My friend Anabel and I are still working on our project for Destiny Day. Extra credit if we do a good job."

He stares like I've just told him I'll be flying to the moon and reporting back. "Anabel? You working with a girl? She's not turning you into a sissy, is she?" Uncle Raymond turns back to his reflection and parts his hair just so, slicking it down with that smelly hair tonic.

"She's my friend, Uncle Raymond." I bite my lip and try again. "Think you'll be around on Destiny Day?"

He reaches out to smooth down a peeling edge of the flag decal he's stuck on the mirror, and only the sound of the air conditioner whirring answers my question. "I ain't got time for any of this," he barks.

"My project's about baseball history."

"Baseball, huh. You know a thing or two about baseball. Sure don't need some girl helping you."

Before I can explain the assignment, Uncle Raymond shuts the door in my face. But yeah, I do want some girl helping me. Even though I totally know about baseball.

To prove it, I reach into the drawer for my thick brown envelope. Two years ago on my birthday, July 20, 1972, my granddaddy took me to see the Braves play the Cardinals. On the long drive from our farm to Atlanta in the rain, he worried the whole way they might call the game. But by the time we got to the stadium, the stars were out.

I pull out my Hank Aaron autographed baseball card,

signed that night. Granddaddy always told me to hang on to it, no matter what.

No matter that my uncle sold every single thing to pay for my grandparents to go to someplace nice. He sold the piano. He sold our furniture. He gave away my dog and most everything else. I slip the card into my pocket. My uncle's not getting this baseball card.

I leave early for school the next morning. On the way out the door, I pass the front hall radiator. Which holds Anabel's mom's basket, pretty much tucked out of sight. Nothing written about putting money in, but everybody who's danced in Miss Sister's classes forever must know the drill. The rest of us don't matter.

Won't hurt to peek inside, will it? Three tens, four ones, two quarters. I'm fastening the little hook, closing the basket up tight, when Mamie appears.

"What're you doing?" she bellows out.

"Nothing." I step away from the radiator.

"You bothering Miss Sister's gift money?"

"No."

Leaving Mamie standing with her hand on her hip and her tongue sticking out, I open the front door and head for Johnson Junior High.

First person I see? Down the sidewalk? Anabel, squashed up next to a giant gardenia bush like she's trying to disappear. "Pssst! Theo! Over here."

"Why're you hiding?"

"I can't go near that place." She nods toward the dance studio. "Remember? I'm avoiding Miss Sister. She thinks I've hurt my foot. Ma's sure I'm gonna be a flapper."

"A flapper?"

"In the stupid dance recital." She steps around the bush. "Those ladies who danced the Charleston a million years ago? Wearing high heels and fringe and feathers." Anabel snorts out a pig-sounding laugh. "I am not letting my mother put feathers in this." She points to her ponytail tied up with a thick band and the shaggy black bangs that cover her eyebrows.

"I may be helping out with the recital," I say.

"Dancing?" Anabel stops and gives me a look. "You want to take my place?"

"Very funny. I'm playing the piano."

She shakes her head, rolls her eyes, and mumbles something about why I'd want to be anywhere near the dance studio for any reason. "You *like* listening to all that music? Nonstop?"

"I like playing the piano. I can learn almost anything I hear. But you can't let on to anybody," I say.

"Why not? Who cares?"

Now we're walking fast down the sidewalk, but I stop and say, "My uncle, for one. He's not too crazy about pianos. Told me I couldn't play."

Since she hasn't fallen on her face laughing, maybe she doesn't mind having a friend who loves to play the piano. Or one whose uncle is just plain mean.

"Your uncle sounds like he'd get along real good with my mom," she says. "Still haven't told her this project doesn't feature baseball players in tap shoes." I laugh at that picture.

Once we're safely away from the Rest Easy, I open my knapsack.

"Found this in the attic. Might be good for our project, but it's locked." I turn the metal box upside down. "See that note taped to the bottom?"

Anabel shakes it. She reads the note. "*Henry?* Get it open, Theo," she says.

I grab a big rock by my foot. Should I do it? It is Miss Sister's, officially. But she probably doesn't even know what's in that attic. Two hard blasts and the lock springs open. "Guess it's pretty old."

"Yeah! Old." She lifts the top and peers inside. "Look! I told you! Proof!"

Two ticket stubs: Braves versus Phillies. 1954. Twenty years ago. A scribbled list of names. Scorecards somebody's filled in.

"Mr. Wyatt's gonna be excited when he sees our research," Anabel says.

I reach into my pocket. "Not sure this is the kind of research we need, but my granddaddy and I got this at a game two years ago. Hank Aaron signed it." I hold up my precious baseball card.

"Wow, Theo. Cool beans." She holds the card next to the handwritten list of names from the box, turning it every which way. "See! On his signature, same *H*s! Got to be Henry Aaron's." Anabel smiles and pushes the metal box my way. "Keep it safe," she says. "We'll work on our project in class. Not at the Rest Easy where you-know-who might see me."

Yeah, I know who. Miss Sister. The one person who can save me from my uncle. Teach me more music. And I'm keeping a secret from her.

I tuck the box into my knapsack and take slow, mostly happy breaths all the way to school.

For the rest of the week, Anabel and I spend every afternoon trying to prove that baseball players really lived in Destiny. She asks her dad, the mayor, a million questions. We sift through Mr. Dawson's stuff, piece by piece. Compare my baseball card signature to anything inside the old tackle box. Do we have enough to ace Mr. Wyatt's social studies project? The way I figure, if I do well in school, I at least have a chance of convincing Uncle Raymond that Destiny is where we belong.

CHAPTER FIFTEEN

Mrs. Johnson Storms the Studio

My uncle snoring, Mr. Hernandez singing in the shower, and the smell of hot biscuits and bacon wake me up early on Saturday. Sitting on the bench outside the studio, I toss my baseball in time to Miss Sister's *shuffle ball change, tap tap tap.* By the time the cuckoo clock finally announces it's eight in the morning, tap shoes echo down the front hall.

"That old air conditioner in my studio had better hold on. My dancers need plenty of kicking and tapping to get ready for their performance." She sinks down next to me, spreading her long flowy skirt every which way and dabbing at her face with a lace handkerchief. "Haven't worked this hard since I was performing on stage myself!"

"Where'd you learn to dance, Miss Sister?" I ask.

"Happy you asked!" She leads me to the wall filled with photographs. "You ever been to New York, Theo?"

"No, ma'am." Then a thought pops into my head. Maybe I have! When I was just a baby. Maybe my mama and daddy took me there to hear that Thelonious Monk guy. Or somebody almost as famous.

Miss Sister straightens a silver frame with a dancer kicking her knees almost up to her nose and points to the dancer. "That's me, a Rockette in New York," she says.

"In that toy soldier costume?" I stare at the picture and yep, it's Miss Sister, not much older than me. "What's a Rockette?"

"Famous dancers at Radio City Music Hall. I was young and fantastic! Swept along at the end of the kick line. During the famous Christmas show, I'd do almost three hundred kicks at each performance." She rubs at a smudge on the glass, then tucks a stray curl into something that looks like fishnet wrapped around her hair.

"I bet you were the best one," I say.

"Well, I've always been on the short side. Some people thought that meant I couldn't be a dancer, but I followed my dream. Oh my stars, all those high kicks. *Up, down, up. Down, out, down.* That's the rhythm." Her fingers skip across the silver frame. "Dancing in New York! My dream."

I know something about dreams.

"Why didn't you stay a Rockette?" I ask.

"Since I was a little bit of a girl, I'd been dancing in Destiny. Always planned to come back, marry my childhood sweet-heart. Teach my own daughter pliés and jetés." She stops to take a breath. "I started out a Rockette, ended up running this dance academy. Never had children, but I've taught most every little girl in town. A few boys, too." She squeezes my hand so tight it hurts. "That's what happens. You start off dreaming one thing about your life. But you have to be ready for what turns up."

"In a million years, I wasn't ready for Uncle Raymond turning up in my life." Looking right at her, I say, "But I'm glad my uncle brought us to the Rest Easy. I hope we don't ever have to leave."

"Me too, honey." This time when Miss Sister smiles, those might be tears squeezing out of her eyes. "Like my own sweet grandmother always said, *Every river needs a bank*. You know what I mean, Theo?"

Like her pillows on the porch glider! All those sayings! But no, I have no clue what that one means.

"Gotta get ready for my dancing queens." She laughs and flounces off. I elbow past a bunch of giggling girls in leotards. Ducking into the kitchen, I grab a bacon biscuit and hurry to hide out in my room.

But upstairs, my uncle's awake, sitting on his bed polishing his shoes so bright they hurt my eyes. "Today's Saturday. Laundry day."

"Yessir," I answer.

He looks around the room, up at the ceiling fan turning slow, out the window. After a while, he puts away his polishing cloth, crosses his arms, and says, "You've done an okay job, keeping up with your chores."

That may be the first halfway nice thing my uncle's ever told me.

"Thanks." I stuff our laundry into the bag and start to smile, but he's already turned his back to me.

Uncle Raymond grabs his tool chest and opens the door. "When's that school of yours over?" he asks, not looking back.

I bite my tongue. I won't mouth off, asking if he's planning to send chocolate cupcakes to celebrate the end of sixth grade. "A week from Monday," I answer, hoping he's not planning on leaving as soon as school's out.

"See you stay out of trouble while I'm at work. Don't forget that laundry."

As he walks down the stairs, I think I hear humming. A song my granddaddy taught me. Right on key. A song about John Henry the Steel Drivin' Man.

Nah. Couldn't be Uncle Raymond.

I'm back at the Rest Easy, about to sneak up the stairs with the clean laundry when Miss Sister bursts out of her dance studio and grabs me by the arm.

"Theo. I could use some help! Right now! Please." Her voice goes up and down, and the dozen bracelets covering her arms rattle and jingle.

I peek around her. Kids who don't appear to be old enough to count, much less count dance beats, surround the piano. No way am I getting trapped in that fluffy cloud of pink cotton candy leotards. "Me? Help?"

"The needle on the record player broke. I don't have time to find another one," she says. "My little dancers are full of beans!"

Unable to come up with a good reason to say no before Miss Sister drags me into the studio, I quickly stash the clean laundry under a bench. Yikes. Little girls cluster so close I can't hardly breathe. When she asked if I wanted to play for her recital, I figured I'd have more time to practice before being thrown to the leotarded wolves. Miss Sister claps her hands, and they stand with their feet together. From the end of the line, Mamie sticks out her tongue. The rest of the girls hold up their arms, making little circles over their heads. Sort of.

"Dancers, this is Theo. He's helping us today." Miss Sister points to me sitting at the piano, about to break out in a cold sweat. "Ready, set. One, two, three." She sings out the words, " 'Shine little glowworm, glimmer, glimmer.' "

When I touch the smooth keys, it all comes back. Miss Sister's shoes tap out the beat in time to my perfect glow-wormy tune. If I forget there are twelve little girls wearing tights and tap shoes two feet away from me, I can do this.

Till Mamie shuffles over and elbows me. "Did you see me twirling?" Just in case I missed it, she spins around, then does another bow.

"Mamie! I seem to be calling your name an awful lot today." Miss Sister holds up her hands, clap-clap-clapping her way across the floor. "In line, tiny tappers!" They start again, but every time Miss Sister shouts out, "Slide to the right!" they shuffle off to the left. "This way! Now, one and two — the other way!"

They all end up smack-dab in the middle. Man, I can see why she needs my help.

But before Miss Sister can line the dancers up again, the studio door bangs open like a fierce wind blowing through. Dressed in pointy high heels and a bright red scarf and sun hat, Anabel's mom stands on the polished dance floor, arms crossed. Her face is lit up the color of the silk scarf wrapped around her neck.

"Miss Grandersole, may I have a word?"

Why's she staring at *me*?

"I'm in the middle of rehearsing," Miss Sister answers. "Please wait outside."

"I cannot wait. This is important." Mrs. Johnson glares. "I prefer to speak in private." Another glare. "Where others can't eavesdrop."

The only *others* in the room are me and a bunch of five-year-olds.

Mrs. Johnson turns on her high heels and sashays out of the room like she rules the dance academy. Miss Sister jabs a long fingernail toward the dancers. "Sit in a circle and listen to Theo!" She follows Mrs. Johnson, shaking her head the whole way.

Through the slightly open door, I see them talking in the front hall. I play soft notes on the piano, trying to ignore the glowwormy noises surrounding me.

But when *Theo Thomas* pops loud out of the whispers in the hall, it stops my music dead still. Daring the glowworms to blink, I move closer to the door.

"I don't want false accusations made against my tenants."

Miss Sister's voice is rising. "Do you have proof it was stolen?"

I can't hear her answer, but Anabel's mom storms off like she's late to a fire and she's the driver of the fire engine. In a quick flash, Miss Sister's back in the studio, smiling. Ready to start dancing again. As if Mrs. Johnson hadn't just waltzed into her front hall and said the words *that boy Theo* and *thief* in the same breath.

After the last dancer finally flitters off, Miss Sister moves close to the piano and says, "I guess you heard. Mrs. Johnson thinks you stole something. She's wrong."

I push my hands in my jeans pockets, clutching my lucky coin.

"She claims you took the money."

I jerk my head up. "Money? What money?"

"That the parents were collecting for a gift. In a little basket closed up tight on the radiator." Miss Sister turns up her nose and jingles her bracelets toward the front hall. "So Beatrice Johnson says."

Anabel's mom thinks I stole *money* from Miss Sister? My whole heart slows down and feels broken. "I didn't take any money."

"That's what I told her. Of course you didn't. Ridiculous!" Miss Sister squeezes my arm, but her dancers are already lining up on the front porch. The show must go on, and all that. I trudge around to the backyard. The notes of "Glow Worm" fade from my memory with each step.

Anabel's waiting by the shed, holding a softball, skipping out on dance class. Again. "Did you see my mother?" she asks.

"I saw her. Talking to Miss Sister." The words stick in my throat, matching up with the knots in my stomach.

Instead of looking at me, she tosses the ball up and down. "She say anything?"

"That I stole the gift money." I jam my fist into my hand. "Don't know why she thinks that."

"I guess 'cause you live here and you're new in town." Anabel leans against the shed and shuts her eyes. "Ma has some crazy ideas about who belongs in Destiny and who doesn't," she says quickly.

"Guess she'd be happy if I left town and never came back." Kind of like my uncle.

"My mom dreamed up the stolen money, right?" A catch in her voice makes me wonder if she's sure about that. When she looks up, she answers her own question. "She dreamed it up. Yeah. But it's okay. If you needed it. I mean, you'd pay the money back, right?"

"I didn't take anything, Anabel." I'm too mad to talk to her. She can disappear from Miss Sister's and I won't even notice. "I gotta go. The next class is coming." I storm off toward the back door, turning to spit out the words, "I don't steal!"

"Wait up, Theo! That's not what I meant." She takes a step toward me. "Meet me Monday after school. We'll finish our baseball project. Together!" she calls out. "Please?"

I shove open the door and don't look back. Some friend Anabel's turning out to be.

When I stop outside the studio door, Miss Sister's next class is sitting on the floor while she rearranges music on the top of the piano. All I want to do is run upstairs and hide in my room, but she sees me.

"Theo? Come in here, please!" I step up close to the piano and she lowers her voice. "Don't you fret a bit about what Mrs. Johnson said. That money will turn up. Stop your worrying this minute." She pats the bench next to her, and I sit down to play the hat dance song.

Right now, that missing money is all I'm thinking about. But when Miss Sister taps out the beat, my fingers dance across the keys. Pretty soon, almost every mean thought floats away on the notes.

CHAPTER SIXTEEN

The Thief

For the rest of the day, I hide in my room.

I'm embarrassed to confess to Uncle Raymond that his relative has been called a thief. And what's worse? My one friend in Destiny thinks I did it. I'm an outcast. All I can do now is change my name and run away from what I thought might be home.

All night, while Uncle Raymond snores happily in the next bed, I stare at the peeling wallpaper. With the moon shining bright through my little window, the pink flowers fade to nothing. Kind of like I'm feeling right about now.

On Sunday, I read my baseball book, cover to cover. By Monday, I have to face the music.

Without saying good-bye or hello to anybody, I slip out of the Rest Easy and into Johnson Junior High. When I open the door to the school's front hall, I want to throw up. All those class pictures may be giving me their fake *Smile for the camera* looks, but the actual kids open up a wide path for me to pass through. It's not my bad haircut or my dorky T-shirt. Nope. Word spreads fast. Theo's a thief. Steer clear of the new kid.

Except Anabel must not have gotten that *steer clear* message. By second period, she's standing at my desk. "You ready to finish our project? Wanna work together after school?"

"Huh? Your mom's actually letting you in the same room with me?" I open my social studies notebook and pretend not to care.

Anabel rolls her eyes. "Ma doesn't know. But I told you, that missing money doesn't mean anything to me."

Not exactly the same as saying she believes me.

I take out my notes, ignoring loud whispers drifting across the room from the kids sketching their manatee mural. But when two girls in the front row look up from gluing leaves onto a fake banyan tree and whisper "Stole a lot of money," a bad stomachache hits me. In my entire life, I've never been to a school nurse. Okay, maybe we didn't even have a nurse at my school in Kentucky. But I've never had a stomachache. Or a reason to pretend I have one. Until now.

"Mr. Wyatt." I raise my hand. "I'm not feeling so great. I need to go home."

"Wait! I'll go with you to the nurse," Anabel says. But I grab my books and dash out without so much as a hall pass. Nobody cares if I'm leaving. Let Anabel work on the project by herself. She needs the extra credit, not me.

Racing up the stairs to my room, I slam the door and collapse on the bed. Loud radio music drowns out the remembered, whispered words of those kids at school. And if Anabel believes I stole that money? I might as well cash in my Hank Aaron baseball card and ride the next bus to somewhere.

Yeah! I'll get it right now! I jerk open the dresser drawer and dig around. Nope. Can't do it. I stuff the envelope holding my baseball card and Granddaddy's postcards back in the drawer. When I slump against the bed, I knock my uncle's lamp crooked. Who cares! I'll toss it out the window. But I straighten the lamp and the dresser tilts forward. Something falls to the floor. *Planning Your Alaska Vacation*. I throw the magazine hard across the room.

A dollar bill floats out.

Then three tens. Three more singles. Two quarters roll across the floor. $34.50. The exact amount of money I'd counted in Mrs. Johnson's basket just before she accused me of stealing it.

CHAPTER SEVENTEEN

What Are Friends For?

All afternoon I play the sick card. When Miss Sister knocks at my door, I moan a pitiful "Come in" and barely open my eyes.

"Theo, honey. You hungry?" she says softly, holding a bowl of Mrs. Hernandez's chicken soup right under my nose. Even though it may be my last meal once all of Destiny discovers my uncle's a thief and we're run out of town, I don't look up. "Anabel's downstairs," she says. "She claims you need to work on your baseball project. I told her you were feeling poorly and not up to studying."

"Anabel's here?" I sit up in bed, maybe too quick for somebody as sick as me. "She's downstairs?" I almost blurt out *at your dance studio where she's vowed she'll never show her face?* Instead, I say, "I don't feel like talking." I flop back on my bed and wait for Miss Sister to leave the soup and leave me alone.

She touches my forehead and says, "Call me if you need anything." Before Miss Sister's out the door good, Mamie sticks her nose and her wild snake hair into my room.

"Why're you in bed?" She steps closer. "Are you sick? Or just sick 'cause you did something terrible? What'd you do? You in trouble?"

I guess the lie about my stealing money hasn't made it to kindergarten yet.

"Shut the door. Leave me alone," I say pitifully.

When Mamie backs into the hall, I turn on the radio again, hoping a baseball game will keep me from thinking about my uncle and that money.

At midnight, Uncle Raymond squeaks open the door into our dark room. I'm in bed, curled up in a ball, still as a mouse playing possum. Except my stomach's really doing flip-flops by now.

When he bangs his leg and lets out a cuss word loud enough to wake the dead, I sit up. Uncle Raymond sinks onto his bed, rubs his shin. "Shoot. This room's so crowded with the two of us in here, can't hardly turn around."

Switching on the dim light near my bed, I say, "I wasn't asleep. Something bad happened at school."

He leans closer, staring a hole through me. "What happened? What'd you do?"

"My friend Anabel's mom accused me of stealing," I answer. "Everybody believes her. Maybe even Anabel."

My uncle stands up and pounds his fist on the dresser. "Stealing? Your granddaddy claimed you were perfect." He narrows his eyes at me, his question a snarl. "Guess you've gone and shown your true self now. What'd you steal?"

"Didn't steal anything. Mrs. Johnson stormed into the dance studio and *said* I took money."

"Dance studio? What were you doing near that piano?"

"Did you even hear me, Uncle Raymond? Don't you care if somebody calls me a thief?" When I look sideways at my uncle, all I see is mad. But I'm madder. "She told Miss Sister I took her gift money from the basket."

The room goes quiet, like every breath of hot summer air's been sucked out. When my uncle turns his back, his shoulders move up and down in a deep breath.

"Well, I got a thing or two to tell her," he says, quieter now. "It ain't right, that too-big-for-her-britches lady accusing you like that. One more reason we won't never be welcome here." Uncle Raymond pulls off his dirty work shirt and flings it into the closet.

I want to tell him that here in Destiny, I was beginning to belong somewhere again. Everything was going good. Until now. Instead, I hold up his magazine and shake it. I shove the money at him and say, "Found this. Hidden in our room."

My uncle starts chewing on his thumbnail. "I needed it," he finally answers. "For a friend."

"A friend? What friend?"

"The one who got me my job, that's who. He's in trouble, needed money quick. He paid me back. I was waiting till nighttime to put it back."

The words that have gnawed a hole in my stomach all day spill out. "You're wrong, Uncle Raymond. *I'm* in trouble. My friend, her mom, and maybe even Miss Sister think I swiped that money. Everybody at school heard. *You* got me in trouble."

"See. That's what's the problem in this two-bit town." Uncle Raymond pounds a fist into his hand. His voice gets louder, and I'm hoping Miss Sister, Mamie, the Hernandezes are all asleep. Or at least not listening outside the door. "First thing people think about. Blame the new boy. Nobody likes us here nohow."

"You didn't think about me when you took Mrs. Johnson's money? That somebody might think I did it?"

"My friend helped me, so I was helping him. Tit for tat. Pays to look out for your buddies. Learned that in the army."

"I guess you didn't learn about looking out for your family in the army." I fall back on my bed. "Nothing about *stealing* in your rule book," I mumble, half to myself.

"Ain't stealing if you put it back." Uncle Raymond slips the money into his shirt pocket. "It's going in that basket right now. I'll explain to Miss Sister tomorrow," he says, pulling the door shut behind him.

So his stupid rules are just for me. No Piano Playing. Homework After School. Laundry on Saturday. Keep Your Business to Yourself. For him, it's different: If you steal, pay it back and everything's A-OK.

I lie there with my fists balled up and my head full till I hear Uncle Raymond open the door. He sits to take off one big work boot and drop it next to the bed.

The other boot slams hard on the floor.

His belt rattles when it hits the chair.

Bedsprings creak.

Soon, my uncle's snoring like nobody's business. But all I can think about is that money. And how I'll never be one of those kids whose class pictures decorate the halls of James

Weldon Johnson Junior High School. Kids who stay put longer than it takes to make a friend and then make her mad.

I hear the clock counting down the minutes, tick-tick-ticking next to my bed all night long. My uncle calls out once, his nightmares acting up. Who cares about him, about his army friend who's more important than me. Pulling my pillow tight over my head, I block out every trace of Uncle Raymond.

CHAPTER EIGHTEEN

My Fair-Weather Friend

When I wake up early the next morning, Uncle Raymond's still sleeping. Good. Don't have to talk to him. Forget about the money he *needed*.

Downstairs, Miss Sister's on the front porch holding a china plate under my nose. "Morning, Theo. You feeling better now?" She hands me a biscuit. "Put some meat on those skinny bones," she says, smiling.

My stomach's too knotted up to take more than a bite, but I grab the hot biscuit. When she reaches up to brush crumbs off my cheek, it's all I can do not to lean into Miss Sister's hand and start bawling like a baby.

"Theo, honey, you're not still worrying about Mrs. Johnson, are you?" she asks. "What that woman thinks doesn't make a dime's worth of difference to me."

Not looking at Miss Sister, I fib, "No, ma'am. I'm

worried about my Destiny Day project. Anabel and I have work to do."

I stand up straight and reach deep to touch the last thing my granddaddy slipped me before I left Kentucky. The flat quarter that stays in my pocket. My good-luck piece. Maybe it will push away all the bad. But for sure I'm not telling Miss Sister about Uncle Raymond and the money. That's his lie to confess to.

"Anything I can help you with?" She takes my hand. "You and your uncle doing all right? That man's as hard to crack as a coconut," she says.

Oh man. If she only knew.

Maybe I should own up about the tackle box inside my knapsack. Tell her I found it in the attic of the Rest Easy. The way I figure it? Taking Miss Sister's box was borrowing something she didn't need. Didn't even know she owned. My uncle stealing her money — that was bad.

"Not now, Miss Sister. Maybe later, thanks." I grab my knapsack and drag myself down the sidewalk to school.

Where Anabel waits under the big jacaranda tree. I'll just drop the tackle box next to her on the bench, let her have it. Take off, never thinking about Destiny's baseball players again. What do I need with a box full of baseball stuff? Do I even need a fair-weather friend like Anabel?

She plucks at a purple blossom that's fallen on the bench. "Hey, Theo. You still mad?" she asks, not looking at me.

"You still believe what your mom said?" I answer.

"I didn't believe her. Really. I promise, Theo. She's always trying to tell me what to do. And with who. But I told Ma you would never steal anything." Anabel takes my arm, pulls me onto the bench next to her, and looks right at me. "Sorry if it sounded that way."

"No big deal," I answer, wishing it were true. "Your mom may have her way anyhow. I may be moving." Or we may be run out of town. "My uncle could be getting a new job. Someplace else."

"Leaving Destiny?" She clutches my arm like she's trying to keep me here forever.

"Nothing's decided. I'll be around for Destiny Day."

"Destiny Day! Almost forgot!" She digs through her knapsack and holds up a dirty, unraveling baseball. "Cool, huh?"

I run my hand over the torn stitching, toss it up and down a couple of times. "Where'd you get this?"

"Behind the Rest Easy, near the toolshed. Proves there were baseball players living there. It's ancient! Bet it's been there twenty years."

"Anabel, a baseball could have been there *one* year and still look like that." I stand up and touch the old tackle box, safe inside my knapsack.

"Well, it's research. Going in our project." She sticks the ball in her own knapsack, and we walk together into school. With Anabel next to me, I don't even notice the faces staring out from those class pictures in the hall.

CHAPTER NINETEEN

All the Good-Luck Pieces in the World

After school, my uncle's sitting on his bed with his tool chest wide open. A baseball game's on the radio, like everything's hunky-dory. But if he hasn't apologized to Miss Sister, I'm not talking.

"Theo." Uncle Raymond nods my way, swishes his rag across his ball-peen hammer, then holds it up to the light, checking for specks of dirt. "School all right today?" He tests the hammer against his hand, popping it once or twice, then moves on to a wrench.

I stand in the doorway, arms crossed.

"You hear me, boy?" he says, his narrowing eyes turning mean.

"School was okay," I mumble.

Just to show him how okay it was, I open a book. He'll

never know it's a book I haven't looked at before and don't need to look at now. Finally, I glance up, asking what we both know needs explaining. "What about Miss Sister? You put that money back and apologize?"

"I spoke to her. We're squared away." My uncle lines up screwdrivers in his big tool chest, tallest and fattest first. He pulls out a sharp knife and scrapes gunk off one before adding it to the chest. "You know, Theo," he says. "You and me gonna stay together, you need to keep out of my business."

"Not if it gets me in trouble I won't."

"Careful how you speak to your elders, boy." Uncle Raymond's tapping that sharp knife against his metal tool chest. *Tap. Tap. Tap.* "Bet you never talked back to your granddaddy like that," he says.

"Granddaddy never did anything wrong." All I hear is the sound of my uncle breathing and the knife dropping against the top of the tool chest. I scoot to the far end of my bed.

Uncle Raymond turns, stands up, and smacks both hands against the dresser hard. "Nothing wrong? How 'bout letting his daughter run off to learn how to be a musician? That's where she learned to carry signs claiming soldiers were nothing but baby killers. Where she and that no-count musician of a husband spit on soldiers, burned the American flag."

"My mama and daddy?" I stare out my window at the afternoon sun, but cold air has slipped into our room, making me shiver. "They wouldn't do that."

"They did it, and worse." His voice cracks with hatefulness. "And your granddaddy didn't do a thing. Didn't tell her she'd better stand up for family. Even if that family was nothing but a army grunt like me."

I'm shaking too hard to answer.

Uncle Raymond's words get louder. "See this here?" He picks up his knife. "This was more help than my sister ever was. Stayed with me every day in Vietnam. A good-luck piece. Kept me safe. Knife this sharp can do some damage."

I push my hand into my pocket to touch my coin.

"Sure didn't have luck after I came back from that war." Now he's almost hollering. "Deserved more respect. So I don't need no mouthing off from you about what I oughta be doing. I took you in because I had to. You're supposed to be family. Start acting like it! You hear me?" He holds the knife up and takes a step toward my bed before jamming it back in its sheath. He bangs closed his tool chest and shoves it under the bed, then takes another step toward me.

Pushing my back hard into the wall, I get as far from my uncle as I can in this little room. But I'm mad, too. I say quietly,

"I'll start acting like family when you prove you are my family."

Uncle Raymond steps closer, poking a dirty fingernail into my forehead, holding it there till it hurts. "I'm all you got, boy. Think about that for a while." And he storms out the door, leaving me shaking on the bed.

At suppertime, I stay in my room and eat stale saltines left from the chicken noodle soup. Music on the radio lulls me to sleep even before it's dark out.

When I wake up the next morning, Uncle Raymond's gone. Or maybe he never came home. What difference does it make? He's changed me from a perfectly normal kid growing up on a farm with grandparents who loved me a lot. Happily riding the school bus with the same friends every day for most of my life. And now? I'm living in a rooming house with an uncle who wishes I hadn't been born.

Slamming my books into my knapsack, I leave for school without making up my bed or even putting away my toothbrush and comb.

CHAPTER TWENTY

Saving Things for Just in Case

All the way home that day, I'm humming "Boogie Woogie Bugle Boy." Maybe my uncle will be waiting for me at the Rest Easy, and everything's back to normal. Whatever that is. Maybe he'll get to know my cool friend who loves baseball. This summer Anabel will teach me to body surf. Me and Uncle Raymond, we'll go fishing and swimming together.

Well, maybe not swimming. And maybe everything *isn't* okay. My stomach tightens up remembering last night.

I round the corner and see Mamie at the mailbox. Again. Holding a piece of fat yellow chalk. "I'm gonna lie down over there now." She points to the sidewalk. "You want to trace me from head to toe?"

"No, thanks."

"Wanna hear a joke? What game do baby fish play? Come on, Theo. Guess."

I don't need to answer.

"Salmon says!"

I don't even smile.

"You sure are being mean to me. Did you tell Miss Sister you robbed her money?"

"You don't know what you're talking about." I keep walking toward the front porch.

"Lying and stealing," she hollers. "You are gonna get in big trouble. Miss Sister'll tan your hide." Then Mamie and her chalk take off.

Inside, I slip into the dance studio and stash my knapsack under the piano bench. Miss Sister's not here, but I open her piano and run my fingers fast up and down the keyboard. If I'm going to master her Destiny Day dance recital numbers, I can't think about my uncle. I can't think about that pest Mamie or Anabel's mom. My fingers are flying. The stolen money, leaving Destiny, all my worries pour out with the music. "Boogie Woogie Bugle Boy" pushes Uncle Raymond clear out of my head.

Miss Sister sways slowly across the polished floor and sits beside me. "Beautiful, Theo! Better than the recording. You're ready to play at the recital."

"Maybe. If Uncle Raymond doesn't haul me out of here before then," I say quietly.

"Your uncle's not taking you anywhere. I'll see to that," Miss Sister says.

Like that's that. Easy peasy. "He told me about looking for a new job."

"Foolishness!" Miss Sister claps her hands together. "Now let's get back to what's important. Playing for the recital. You'll be my first live piano man!" She listens while I hit the fast notes, swaying, her eyes closed, smiling at me.

But something still swirling in my head pushes the music away. "I found something in your attic," I say, leaning down to open my knapsack. "I took it."

Her eyebrows go straight up. "Nothing up there but dust, spiderwebs, and faded costumes."

"This was beside a trunk pushed in the corner." I pull out the tackle box and show her the photographs, the ticket stubs. "Anabel and I need it for our baseball history project."

"Glad to hear that girl's up to something good. She's usually just figuring out ways to skip out of dance class." Miss Sister winks.

"I'm sorry I went in your attic without asking. Mr. Dawson at the bait shop told us baseball players could have lived here." I hold up the lists and the notes from the box. "I'll give it back."

"What do I need with that? If you think this was the place, I might even find you some old photos of the Rest Easy."

"Thanks, Miss Sister," I say. "We have to explain our project at Destiny Day."

"My, my. You're going to be busy. Destiny Day in the morning down at the square. In the afternoon, star musician of our dance recital." Miss Sister smiles right at me. "Your uncle will be so proud."

I chew my fingernail, then spit it out. "I'm not telling him about the recital."

She wrinkles her nose into a frown. "He'll want to be there. It's your big day, Theo."

"Yeah, right." I grab my knapsack. "Uncle Raymond won't come," I say, and I stomp up the stairs, fast and loud.

It's way past my bedtime and I'm in my room worrying why there's no sign of my uncle.

So I'll clean out our closet.

Dress shirts on one side, work shirts on the other. I'm sorting and organizing, thinking about what to say when he shows up. *I'm still mad about the stolen money, but I'm sorry I was disrespectful.* I carefully put the Destiny Day Baseball Project folder in my knapsack, ready for tomorrow. *Just in case you're wondering, I'm the star musician of the dance recital. Well, that's what Miss Sister says.* My jeans are perfectly stacked up in a basket. Shorts folded on the bottom shelf. *You want to come? What d'ya think,*

Uncle Raymond? My old jacket's stuffed way in the back of the closet. *It'll be fun. Miss Sister and I think you should be there.*

He'll just say no.

I pull out that puke-green jacket I hauled to Florida from Kentucky, and I try it on. Still way too small. Before I stash it back in the closet — saving it for *just in case* like my uncle said — I fiddle with the big ugly buttons on the front. Inside a pocket, something's stuck in the seam. The scrap of paper from my granddaddy's desk. I thought I'd lost it! Granddaddy'd saved the grocery list to remember my mom's handwriting. Just before we left, he gave it to me. Unfolding the little square, I spread it out to read.

Milk, eggs, Cheerios, baking soda.
Chocolate milk for Theo.
Carrots. Dish detergent.

Running my fingers over the words *Chocolate milk for Theo*, I put it with my important things inside the brown envelope in my top drawer.

Then I turn the radio to our station, real quiet. I climb under my sheets, leaving the light on for my uncle. The Braves are winning, 9–2.

CHAPTER TWENTY-ONE

Get Home before the Streetlights Come On

When the clock's alarm blasts the next morning, I wake up with a crick in my neck and some guy on the radio announcing rain's coming. I sit straight up and look around. Nobody's snoring to wake up the dead like usual. Uncle Raymond's bed's made up tight, same as every morning. No work boots under the chair.

My uncle didn't come home again last night. I'm not telling a soul.

I'm out the door and the first one at school, not wanting to think about where he might be. If he's ever coming back. Whether he's hurt or sick or mad. Or just plain giving up.

By last period, I wait for the bell to ring, drumming my fingers in time with that shuffle-ball-change thing running through my head. Trying to push worry about Uncle Raymond out.

When Anabel taps me on the shoulder, I jump a mile. "The bell, Theo? Class is over. Meet me outside." She lowers her voice to a whisper. "I need your help figuring out how to cut out of the dance recital. Without my mom finding out."

I catch up with her under the shady tree at the bus loop. The wind's picked up. A few fat raindrops are starting.

"Tell Miss Sister I was sick and won't be well for dance class on Saturday," Anabel says. "And you heard I'm not getting better anytime soon. Please."

"Can't lie to Miss Sister."

"Well, I'm not going near her dance studio. Come to my house. We can finish our project there," she says.

"All we have left is gluing a few things and figuring out what we're saying at Destiny Day. We can do that at school. I need to get home before the storm hits." I don't wait for her answer before hurrying to the Rest Easy. Where I'm sure Uncle Raymond will be waiting.

Except he's not. Not in our room. Not out back cleaning his tools at the water hose. Not talking to Miss Sister on the porch. Nowhere. Not even a note saying he'll be late from work and for me to eat supper without him.

When the sky opens up and bright flashes of light are followed by thunder so loud my teeth hurt, I wonder if my uncle is safe inside someplace.

*　　*　　*

On Friday morning, I sneak down the stairs and hear Miss Sister playing quiet music. I'm still afraid to tell her Uncle Raymond's gone. I want my life to be what it was before Mrs. Johnson stormed in here accusing me of stealing what my uncle happened to have stashed in our room. Maybe what I want is my life before we ever moved to Destiny, Florida.

Ginger Rogers lifts her head when I slip out the front door. She doesn't bark. Geez. I'm not even important enough for a dog to notice. I push my way through the heat to school.

In social studies, Anabel and I sit next to each other, showing off our project. When kids stop by to admire our raggedy old baseball, the tackle box, the photos and maps, I almost forget about Uncle Raymond. Nobody's saying "Hey, Theo, good work," but they don't whisper "Theo the thief," either. By the time the last girl moves back to her desk to line up her colored pencils, I'm finally smiling.

I'm still smiling when Anabel stops pawing through her research notes and asks, "What color Braves T-shirt are you wearing to Destiny Day? Do you think we should match?"

Huh? Braves T-shirt?

"Don't have one," I answer.

Her eyes open wide. "You don't have a Braves T-shirt? What were you thinking we'd wear?"

"Flapper dress?" I joke.

"That's not funny, Theo. I'm not dancing in the recital. I'm not wearing feathers, tap shoes, or any of that stuff my mom's at home creating right about now." Anabel swallows hard and chews on her lip. "They sell T-shirts at that store out on the highway," she says. "Tomorrow's Saturday. Can your uncle take you?"

I take a deep breath, squirm around in my desk, then lower my voice. "My uncle works most Saturdays," I say. "We don't have a car."

"Really? No car?"

"And my uncle would never buy me a brand-new shirt, especially for a school project." I try to think of a snappy joke. Nothing's coming.

Anabel leans over our carefully drawn map of Destiny, studying each street intersection. "Why do you live with your uncle?" she asks, not looking up.

"It's a long story. Involving grandparents." I doodle on a piece of scratch paper, showing her it's no big deal. When really it's the biggest deal of my entire life. "But I definitely won't be buying a Braves T-shirt."

She pastes the map on our poster board and closes her notebook. "You can wear one of mine," she says, smiling right at me.

As long as Anabel's T-shirt isn't pink and sparkly, I'm not too proud to borrow.

The rest of the day's pretty much a bust. By the time the last bell rings on Friday, we've learned everything there is to know in sixth grade at Johnson Junior High. One more day of school. Monday's mostly parties and picnics to end the year. Tuesday is Destiny Day and the dance recital. Everything happens next week. I hope I'm around to see it.

CHAPTER TWENTY-TWO

Family Sticks Together

ncle Raymond's still missing.

So when I get home from school, I slip into the Rest Easy's kitchen, grab three slices of Wonder Bread, and head down the hall toward the studio. Inside, Miss Sister's playing soft music, too busy worrying over her dance recital to notice my uncle's gone. I touch the door handle, giving it and me a little push. Should I tell Miss Sister he just up and left? And may never come back? Who'll I live with? Where will I go? I need to find Uncle Raymond!

I race off toward Main Street. At the bus stop, a silver Trailways pulls away — maybe the same bus we rode all the way from Kentucky just three weeks ago. One old guy's standing on the sidewalk holding his suitcase. Not my uncle.

Before I cross the street, I quickly check the tree for green parrots. None. I peer in the Chat 'n' Chew's big glass window.

Uncle Raymond's not there, either. Sinking onto the bench in front of the cafe, I take deep breaths, but the deeper I breathe, the more I worry. And if anybody sees me sitting in the middle of Destiny gasping like a crazy person, I'll be sent off to loony land for sure. I jam my hand in my pocket and squeeze my good-luck piece. The coin's not working.

When I take another breath, the smell of water and sunshine slows my heart, bringing back a memory of the day Anabel and I walked to the beach. My uncle would never go there, would he? He's the one who said one look at the gulf was enough.

But where else can I go? I head for the water, sit on the seawall, and pinch off squares of bread. I toss one to a squawking gull, one bite for me, till it's finished. Stepping onto the beach, I throw up my arms and yell at the top of my lungs at the gulls swooping, searching for food. The birds take off. My uncle's still nowhere to be seen, but I feel better.

I might as well head back. Face the music. Tell Miss Sister I'm an orphan. Abandoned. I start toward the wood-planked walk. Wait a minute! Who's that? Out past the gulls fighting over the last crust of bread? Uncle Raymond. Strolling up the walk like nothing happened, like he didn't go off and leave me alone and scared at the Rest Easy.

"I been looking for you." My uncle pulls on the brim of his cap, shielding the afternoon sun.

"You've been looking for me?" I'm hollering so loud the gulls scatter. A little girl playing in the sand runs to her mother. Fishermen stop casting to stare. I don't care. He deserted me! "Where'd you go?"

"Nowhere," he mumbles. "Just needed to leave. I ain't cut out for the family life."

Staring at my uncle like I wish I could haul off and slug him, I say, "Didn't you think about telling me?"

"None of your business where I go, boy. Destiny ain't the only town in Florida. Not even the best one," he yells back. "Army taught me a lot more than changing tires. I worked hard in Alaska. Made good money. I can find me a better job." Before Uncle Raymond stuffs his hands in his pockets, I see he's gnawed his fingernails to the quick since he left.

"You brought me here. I didn't want to come!" By now a fisherman is inching toward the pay phone on the dock like he's about to call the police. Trying to stay calm, I say, "I like Destiny. I don't want to leave."

"I don't know nothing about kids. Especially one that reminds me of the bad times."

"The bad times?" I almost turn around and run all the way back to Miss Sister.

"Every time I look at you, your mama comes back. Not the good parts, either." The cloud covering Uncle Raymond's face is as dark as the storm starting out past the waves. "The bad's your daddy's fault. He got her in with them war protesters! Called me an ignorant murderer, to my mama no less. Telling my own family it was wrong to join the army."

"Granddaddy showed me your medals. He said you were a hero."

"Your mama and me, we were raised to salute the flag, not burn it. But your daddy, naw — both of them, they hated me for going to Vietnam. I signed up twice! When I finally came home, draft dodgers spit on me. I didn't care. I was proud."

"So that makes you hate me?" I whisper the word *hate*. Granddaddy told me never to say it. I wish I didn't have to.

"I hate everything that happened. My mama and daddy having to give up their farm. Your grandparents loved that place." His voice gets quiet. "I hate you having nobody but me," he says slowly. Uncle Raymond stares out at the wide fishnets tossed in circles and the pelicans dive-bombing for dinner.

"Why'd you take me in? I'd be better off in some foster home, where people are paid to care." The wind's picked up, and I rub my arms to fend off the chill.

We turn to face each other. Our arms crossed over our chests, just alike. Except we're more like those gulls out there fighting for fish. Swooping in on top of each other, flying close, then away, circling in different directions.

"You gonna answer or not?" I turn my back to him, brushing something — maybe it's water spray, maybe it's tears — from my face. "Why'd you even want me?"

"*Want* wasn't part of it." His voice rises over the wind. He grabs my shoulder and turns me to face him. "Once I left the farm behind, I didn't need family, didn't think I ever would," he says.

"Family? We never even heard from you, much less saw you. All those Christmases, once I was old enough to understand what an uncle even was. Heard I had one, lived way off in Alaska. Maybe he'd come home this year. Maybe the next. You never did." I kick at the sand and don't care if it blows in my uncle's eyes.

"I ain't done good by anybody, especially you. A boy needs roots." My uncle sucks his breath in and shakes his head. "Me and your mama had roots."

Questions I've wanted to ask since we left Kentucky pour out. "Why won't you ever talk about her? She was your sister. Didn't you love her?"

Uncle Raymond leans against the seawall and I stand next

to him. The clouds off in the distance are still worrying up a rainstorm, but I'm not leaving till I hear everything.

"I was fighting for my country. People like her and your daddy — good-for-nothing peaceniks — were fighting against me. He burned his draft card while I was sitting in some foxhole getting shot at. I vowed I'd never speak to either one of them."

"That's why you don't want me?" My words are almost covered up by the wind.

"After the car wreck, I felt bad. But they made their bed, they had to lie in it." Uncle Raymond's voice is barely a whisper. He moves closer and touches my arm. "But now I'm getting to know you, maybe things can be different. You're my boy."

I jerk back. Maybe something's different for him. Maybe I'm *his boy*. But does he really know me? "If things are different, that means I can play the piano." I look up just as a tiny sliver of sun peeks out from the dark cloud. "Miss Sister thinks I'm good."

"I know you've been sneaking off to Miss Grandersole's piano. But I can't bear listening." Uncle Raymond takes off his hat, fiddles with it, then pushes his hair back and turns to face the gulf. "Music reminds me of the farm, how I took off, left everything I knew. Never had anybody again. Not much of a good memory."

When he stops talking, I pull out my good-luck piece and hand it to my uncle. "Granddaddy gave me this. Almost all I got to remember the farm and my mama by." I don't mention the grocery list in her handwriting. That's just for me. "Granddaddy said when she was my age, Mama carried it everywhere."

Uncle Raymond turns the flat coin over in his palm, tosses it up and down. "Well, I swan. Forgot all about this. My old guitar pick. When I got me a real pick, gave this to your mama." He hands my coin back to me. "Always claimed it brought her good luck. Some good luck it turned out to be."

I stare at my uncle. "You play the guitar?"

"Not no more I don't." His voice is barely a whisper over the gusting wind and the squawking gulls.

I rub the smooth coin, maybe for luck, maybe looking for a memory. "Granddaddy drilled a hole in it so my mama could wear it around her neck."

"Don't you go wearing no jewelry around your neck."

I narrow my eyes at Uncle Raymond.

"Well, maybe this," he says, finally smiling.

"Didn't Mama learn to play the piano at church? Same as me?" I ask.

His voice gets stronger. "She was just a little bitty thing. We got the church's old piano, when they got something better. Before long, your mama gave your granddaddy the what-for — the durn thing was so out of tune. Had some key stuck, couldn't make it work for the life of her." Now he laughs out loud, and it may be the first time I've heard my uncle laugh like that. "Claimed it was in every song she tried to play."

"Not a bad note on Miss Sister's piano," I answer.

Uncle Raymond raises his eyebrows at *Miss Sister's piano*. "Son, we're family now," he says. "We need to stick together. But if we stay at the Rest Easy, the piano playing goes."

My uncle may say we're family. But if he doesn't let me play Miss Sister's piano, he's wrong. When a cool drizzle starts, I shiver, rubbing the ugly scar on my arm. He puts his big hand on my shoulder and squeezes it tight all the way back to the Rest Easy. Just as we step onto the front porch, the skies open up.

CHAPTER TWENTY-THREE

Miss Sister Spills the Beans

The next morning, I wake up early and the coast is clear. My uncle's left for work. He even left me a scribbled note reminding me it's laundry day. But before Miss Sister's dancers arrive, before I even think about dirty laundry, today's my last chance to get every recital piece perfect.

Scooting the piano bench back a few inches, I stretch my foot toward the pedal and warm up with a jazzy piece I heard on Mr. Hernandez's radio. My fingers run from one end of the keyboard to the other, making the tune jump around. "Glow Worm," "Boogie Woogie Bugle Boy," the hat dance — I know my songs as good as I know my own name. I'm ready for anything!

Anything except Uncle Raymond staring a hole through me. My uncle, who was supposed to be busy at the One-Stop Tire Shop all morning, stands tall, right next to me.

He slaps his hat against the piano. His voice cuts through the music in my head. "Were you playing this thing?"

For a half second, I think about telling a big fat lie.

No, Uncle Raymond. That was Miss Sister's recording.

I didn't hear anything. You dreamed it up.

Somebody else was playing this piano. Somebody who disappeared into thin air.

It was the dog.

It was the wind.

It was nobody.

Instead, I bang the keyboard cover closed and say, "What are you doing back so soon?"

"My own business!" He slams his hat harder against the piano. "Didn't you remember what I said yesterday?"

"I remember. Just don't think I can help it."

"Guess you and me, we'll never see eye to eye." Uncle Raymond turns to leave.

"Music's gonna take us apart, just like it did you and your family. Don't you care?" My shout echoes across the bare wood floors.

"Can't live someplace there's music playing all day," he yells back.

"I can't live without music," I answer. I open the piano and play — loud and fast. I end with a big chord, stretching my hands and holding the notes. When I finish, I stand up, and dare my uncle to tell me No Piano Playing Ever.

Shaking his head, Uncle Raymond marches toward the door. Where Miss Sister's standing. Smiling like the two of us hadn't been hollering about her piano being the worst thing that could happen to us.

"You listening to that beautiful music Theo makes?" she asks.

"I told him, we stay here, he can't play no piano," my uncle mutters.

"What poppycock! Theo's music is part of him. He's playing for my recital on Tuesday." Miss Sister flaps her hand at my uncle, hushing him up.

Yesterday's rain or standing next to somebody whose No Piano Playing rule hasn't changed or hearing Miss Sister spill those beans — something in here makes it hard to breathe.

"Theo's the star of my show! You're gonna love hearing him play!" She sidles up to the piano and squeezes my arm. "We'll reserve a seat for you!" she says, smiling at my uncle.

Oh boy. Now I'm in trouble.

When Uncle Raymond storms out, his heavy boots nearly shake down the tall studio mirrors. All I can do is lay my head next to the piano music and cover it with my arms. My uncle at her dance recital. This is never going to work.

CHAPTER TWENTY-FOUR

Destiny Day

For the rest of the weekend, Uncle Raymond and I only speak to each other when he can't find the toothpaste.

On Monday, I escape to school, where we mostly eat cupcakes and drink punch, celebrating summer coming. Just for fun, our English teacher gives us one more shot at turning diagramming sentences into a game. By the last class of the day — surprise — it's like most every day since we moved to Florida. Hot and sticky with a chance of rain. Not a whiff of air moves the palmettos outside the window, and the air conditioner churns out something that smells as musty as my granddaddy's storm cellar. The guys have their heads resting on their desks. The girls slide notes across the aisles. Boring blah blah blah.

Nobody in the history of the universe ever learned one single fact worth knowing on the last day of school.

When I wake up on Tuesday morning, Uncle Raymond's already left for work. Destiny Day and recital music swirling in my head, I throw the covers off and head downstairs just as the hall phone rings. Miss Sister listens, then slams it down.

"Anabel! Claiming she's sicker than a dog and something about an injury. Humph. That child has been wheedling out of dance practice since she figured out what a baseball bat was good for." Miss Sister raises her eyebrows in a question, but I'm not lying about Anabel's sore throat, sprained toe, or whatever else she's dreamed up to skip out of the recital. And she'd better be at our Destiny Day booth.

I hotfoot it upstairs to grab my poster and notes and slip on Anabel's Braves T-shirt. Not bad, Theo! Red's my color.

Pretty soon, I'm standing on the corner near the Chat 'n' Chew, eyeing the trees for birds and the sidewalk for Anabel. She's opening a card table in front of the post office.

"Miss Sister's mad," I say. "But I didn't tell her anything."

"No great loss. I was the klutziest flapper known to man." Anabel straightens out the blue-and-white tablecloth and lines up our report's pages. Her foot's wrapped in a bandage, but her fake sore throat seems loud as ever.

I look behind me, down Main Street. "Whoa! Wait a minute. Where'd all these weird-looking strangers come from?" I ask.

When I went to bed last night, it was sleepy little Destiny, population maybe four thousand. This morning, Main Street's filled with old guys dressed as soldiers and ladies who look like they lived when people washed their clothes in a river. Forced kids to pick berries to eat. Cooked hot dogs over a fire. Okay, scratch the hot dog thing. It *was* a hundred years ago.

"Destiny, Theo. We're celebrating the town's history. Remember?" Anabel's tacking red, white, and blue crepe paper around our table. "Hold this." She hands me a wide banner announcing *Destiny, Florida: Home of the Brave(s)!*

I point to the Brave(s) thing and laugh. "Good one, Anabel."

"My mother came up with the tablecloth. Be sure to notice." Anabel rolls her eyes. "Lucky you, only an uncle. I bet he doesn't butt into your business."

I have no answer for that.

When Mamie shows up waving cotton candy big as a balloon, she stands with one hand on her hip staring at the old baseball. "What's all this junk?" she asks.

"Not junk. Proof that famous baseball players lived in Destiny," I say. "Henry Aaron, for starters."

"What's so great about him?"

"Broke Babe Ruth's record," I answer. Like she'd even know who that is.

"Know any baseball jokes?" she says, reaching out with cotton candy hands to touch my special Hank Aaron card.

Anabel shoots Mamie her best evil eye. "No touching. Just looking," she says.

Mamie glances at our poster, then sticks out her tongue. Before I can impress her with more baseball facts or listen to a stupid baseball joke, Mr. Wyatt shows up and Mamie moves to the next table.

"The baseball project! Let's see what you got here." Anabel starts in with the stories about Henry Aaron and his friends walking on the beach, eating at the Chat 'n' Chew, fishing with Mr. Dawson's shrimp bait. How Destiny was the spring training home of famous baseball players. The way she's talking, I expect Aaron himself to saunter up and share his home run stats. Mr. Wyatt listens politely, then asks, "You can prove they lived here?" We look at each other.

"Sure!" Anabel smiles real big. "Well, mostly. Here's our report for the historical people. In perpetuity. Or whatever that word was."

He traces a finger across the map I've intricately drawn and labeled. "Good work here, Theo," he says.

"Mr. Dawson at the bait shop remembered some of the players." I point to the list on our big poster. "Miss Sister gave us old photographs of the Rest Easy. Anabel took pictures of the marks on the toolshed there. Probably from somebody with a strong arm tossing a baseball."

Or maybe me tossing fuzzy tennis balls, I don't say.

"Extra credit for both of you! I'll hand this off to the Historical Society." Mr. Wyatt collects our research report and moves on.

By two o'clock, maybe the crowds have had too much sun, too much food, or they've heard all they need to know about One Hundred Years of the Town Time Forgot. The loud-speaker guy loops his long electrical cord back onto the machine. The tuba band stops playing. The cotton candy seller hands out free samples, then packs up his machine. Destiny Day is dying down.

"Still aren't coming to the recital?" I ask Anabel. "I'm playing."

"Sorry, Theo. No can do. Much as I'd like to hear you, I need to stay clear of that auditorium."

"What about your mom? You lie to her like you did to Miss Sister?"

"My mom knows nothing." Anabel points to her foot. "I only put the bandage on in case Miss Sister showed up here." She clears her throat and coughs. "I feel a bad cold coming on. Mom will understand. If she even makes it to the recital." She smiles and tosses our old baseball up and down.

"You're kidding, right? Mrs. Johnson, not at the recital? After collecting the money for Miss Sister?" And accusing me of stealing it. But I'm over that. The mystery was solved. I'm off the hook. My uncle put it back and apologized to Miss Sister, who spread around a cockamamie story about finding it behind the radiator.

"Mom's already handed off the gift thing. Mamie's presenting the flowers." Anabel coughs again, then looks around to see who's heard her. "I may have mentioned to her and my dad that the recital was changed to seven tonight," she whispers. "Seven sharp." She grins. I shake my head.

"The recital starts at five."

"I know that. But it's a busy day. What my mom doesn't figure out won't hurt her. Or me."

"Dream on, Anabel," I say.

"Ma's too busy running Destiny Day. Daddy, too. They've forgotten all about me."

Anabel's parents have forgotten about her about as much as Uncle Raymond has remembered he was invited to the recital.

Together, we take down our poster. Fold up the card table and stash it against a palm tree. "My dad'll be by to pick this up. You go ahead." She hands me the tackle box and my special baseball card. "Take good care of Hank Aaron's autograph.

I'm sure it got me a good grade. See you later? Ice-cream stand after supper?"

"Unless you're grounded for life," I say.

"Not a chance!" Anabel smiles. "And, Theo? Let's think of something to do together over the summer. The beach? Bug Mr. Dawson to give us free bait crickets? Learn to surf? You will be here this summer, right?"

"Maybe," I say.

Yep. I hope I'm here. But I'm having trouble thinking about summer. My stomach's beginning to knot up and I didn't even eat the cotton candy or fried dough.

I run all the way back to the Rest Easy, sure I'm breaking another one of my uncle's rules, like Never Run When You're Worried. Before heading upstairs, I poke my nose into the dance studio, just to say hello to my piano.

CHAPTER TWENTY-FIVE

The Stage Is Set

For the next hour, I lie collapsed across my bed, staring first at the clock, then at the chipped ceiling paint. Wiggling glowworms dance like all get-out in my belly. But at exactly 4:20 I hear somebody banging around in the front hall. I take the steps two at a time and almost crash into Miss Sister carrying a basket of something feathery.

"Oh my. Always something left to the last minute. Need to get back to the auditorium. See you there!" She hurries to her car and drives off in a swirl of red streamers and fake palm fronds.

Bummer. I was hoping for a last-minute pep talk.

I tuck my ironed dress shirt into my jeans just as Mr. Hernandez appears. "Break a leg, Theo!" he calls out. Which reminds me of Anabel and her mom. Great.

Good thing Johnson Junior High School is just down the

street, because it's about five hundred degrees and the white-hot sidewalk almost knocks me over. Will I pass out before the curtain even goes up? Hoping my sneakers don't stick to the bubbling tar, I cross the parking lot and open the side door into the auditorium.

"Oh my stars! These tappers move around more than a flea on a dog." Miss Sister waves her clipboard at the dancers. "Quiet! We have an audience out there."

Oh yeah. The audience. I swallow the tightness in my throat.

"Here's your program," she says. "Got your name right on it! Hope your uncle's here to see this!"

In your dreams, Miss Sister.

I open the folded white paper. Little American flags decorate the front.

MISS SANDRA GRANDERSOLE'S TAP AND BALLET RECITAL

IN HONOR OF OUR TOWN'S 100TH ANNIVERSARY

AND ITS DESTINY

JUNE 11, 1974

THELONIOUS MONK THOMAS, ACCOMPANIST

Yikes. My name, my real name. Right there for the world to see.

Hey. It looks pretty cool.

Miss Sister swirls around, then fiddles with the fat beads circling her neck. "Like to get all fancied up," she says. When she shakes out her skirt, sequins catch the light. "Now, Theo honey, I expect you'll want to come out at the end and take a bow, maybe cut a rug with me. The children might even have a little something for you."

Okay. Now I know I'll faint. Or worse.

She taps a long red fingernail at my chest and smiles. "You're up first. You and the glowworms. Get out there and tear that piano to pieces." She moves toward the rope that opens the big curtain.

From the auditorium wing, I peek out. Man, people are so close, one false note and they're onto me. What a fake I am! I've never played the piano in front of an audience. Well, nobody but the preacher and our church. Nobody who cared if I missed a note.

Sweat pours down my back. A gazillion parents must be holding their noses at my BO. I try not to stare at the waving cameras. Wait! Is that Mrs. Johnson, Anabel's mom, *smack-dab in the front row*? Close enough to stand up and knock the music off the shiny black piano or even slam it closed? She's not supposed to be here.

Why had I thought this was a good idea?

I clutch my sheet music. Not that I need the music. I can't hardly read music! I can play my three songs with my eyes closed. Or tossing a baseball. In my sleep. *Deep breaths, Theo. You can do this.* I take the six steps across the stage on feet as heavy as the piano bench. *Please don't let me faint and fall on my face. Please don't let me trip on the floor lights. Please.*

The curtains open and Miss Sister starts talking before I find middle C on the upright piano. "Welcome to our dance recital. This year's theme is Destiny's History." I think she says something about the first number, but my heart's pounding so loud it drowns out everything. Oh, why can't I be that black lizard from the Rest Easy's porch railing and blend into the piano bench right about now?

Miss Sister looks right at me. "Ready, maestro?" she says, and disappears into the wings.

Miraculously, my hands hit the right keys, and a line of little girls dressed in green leotards and tights hold each other by their waists and snake across the stage. I'm not sure what glowworms have to do with the history of Destiny, but I'm sure Miss Sister has that covered. Not counting the girl who stands off to one corner of the stage waving at her mother, the Tiny Tapper Glowworms perform without a mistake. I play the last chord. The curtains close. The lights go dark. Miss

Sister scoots a fake palm tree off to one side of the stage, clicks her fingers for the next number, and I finally breathe.

Till I hear somebody in the audience whispering, loud.

"I can't believe Miss Sister allows that boy in the recital. What is she thinking? He's nothing but a bad influence. He and that uncle."

My ears burn red-hot. I dig my nails into my hands. Even with the curtain closed, I know. It's Anabel's mom.

The curtains open and I glance back. She's looking around, twisting her neck like a flamingo. She might as well be on the stage when she announces to her entire row, "Anabel's with the flappers waiting for her grand entrance. I sewed the feathers into her headpiece myself."

Oh man. By now Anabel has ditched her feathered and fringed costume and is a million miles from the auditorium.

As the lights come up again, I sneak a better look. The way Mrs. Johnson's dressed, she might be going to see those Rockette dancers in New York City. A fancy hat covers up her jet-black hair. White gloves pinch her hands as tight as water balloons.

Water balloons! If only I had one about now, Mrs. Johnson would be history.

She catches my eye and glares. But I breathe in and out, turning my breaths into music beats. I focus on a sliver of brightness falling on the keyboard from the piano light and think about harmony. Once the first note sings out, nothing matters but the rhythm of tap shoes matching my bass chords. Me and my piano in perfect time with Mexican hat dancers shuffle-tapping on stage. *Shuffle shuffle. Heel toe heel.*

Three more dances, set to recordings, then my last number.

"'Boogie Woogie Bugle Boy.' To honor our World War II veterans," Miss Sister announces.

I play without one mistake, wipe my hands on my jeans, and can't stop the grin that sneaks up. I want to lean over and kiss the keyboard!

When the lights go down again, I slide off the piano bench before girls in swishy skirts dance out to their flapper record. I'm outta here before Mrs. Johnson beams that fake smile toward the stage and doesn't see Anabel. Don't need to be around for those fireworks. Or for the grand finale. Miss Sister will do a kick or two from her Rockette days. The glowworms will prance across the stage with flowers. Maybe some for me. Who cares about flowers. I'm sure not coming out and *cutting a rug* with Miss Sister.

Okay. Maybe just one look.

Backstage, Miss Sister's holding a crepe-paper torch and wearing a red, white, and blue cape. She's the Statue of Liberty, surrounded by all the flappers except one. I back out toward the door to escape.

"Hey, Theo!"

Busted. Mamie sees me and grabs my hand. Pulling me onto the edge of the stage, she hands me one rose.

"You did really good," she whispers. I'm sure my cheeks match the red rose.

Now everybody on stage claps and cheers, swaying to the recording of "When the Saints Go Marching In." Mamie and another glowworm present Miss Sister with the whole bouquet of flowers. The audience stands, shouting, "Brava! Miss Sister!"

Everybody but Anabel's mom. Mrs. Johnson's sitting dead still. Right there in the front, arms crossed, eyes squinted together tight.

I can't leave fast enough. Pushing open the side door, I step into late afternoon sun so hot, cars should be sizzling on the blacktop. The air's too heavy to move an empty potato chip bag dropped on the ground. Clutching my rose, I try to catch my breath.

Then I see him. Off to the side of the parking lot holding his hat, dressed in a clean uniform, my uncle lifts his hand, frowns, and waves just a little.

He heard me play. I'm in big trouble now.

CHAPTER TWENTY-SIX

Too Hot to Breathe

*J*ust as I'm deciding to make a break for it, Uncle Raymond walks over. I hop back. But he reaches out and hugs me. My uncle, hugging anybody. Wow.

"Looking good, Uncle Raymond. Even got your name on a new shirt!" I point to the patch: *Raymond*, sewn in script over his pocket.

"Boss gave it to me today. Guess the boys at work want me to stick around." He ducks his head and kicks a rock on the blacktop, then blurts out, "They told me I could leave early. To hear this music for myself."

I shove my hands in my pockets and clutch my good-luck charm in one fist. "Thanks for coming."

"Let's walk back to the Rest Easy. We need to talk," he says. He hasn't smiled since that half hug, so I'm not sure what he'll say. Other than *Yeah, that sounded nice,* but *No Piano Playing Ever Again*. He's already said that a few times.

We're turning the corner at the edge of the parking lot when I see somebody behind those big poisonous bushes Mr. Hernandez warned me about.

"Theo. Pssst. Over here." Anabel's crouched behind the sticky, itchy red flowers, dressed in cutoff jeans and one sneaker. With about a mile of tape wrapped around her bare foot.

"Anabel?" I say. "Shouldn't you be hiding better?"

She peeps out from the oleander bushes. "Wanted to hear how your music was. Congratulate you." She taps her bandaged foot. "If Miss Sister sees me, here's my excuse."

Then I remember. "This is Uncle Raymond, Anabel." Turning from my uncle to my friend, I don't even try to explain one to the other.

"Nice to meet you." When Uncle Raymond reaches out to shake her hand, I notice he's cleaned the dirt out from under his fingernails to match his spotless uniform shirt.

"Did you hear Theo play? He's really good. Or so I hear. I missed his big day." Anabel points to her foot again. Uncle Raymond nods instead of answering.

Now the crowd's starting to pour out. Happy noises spread over the parking lot. I look at Anabel and say, "You better get out of here. Your mom's gonna find out you ditched the recital. Miss Sister, too."

"My mom'll get over it. But she won't realize I wasn't dancing like some idiot flapper girl till I confess and explain I'm never dancing again," she says, like she's solved her lifetime tap-dancing problem.

"She was sitting in the first row, center aisle," I tell her. "Breathing down my neck."

"Yikes." Anabel turns, ready to run with a fake broken toe and one sneaker missing. She stops and glances back toward the auditorium. "Maybe she didn't notice I wasn't there?" she asks.

"She noticed," I answer.

"I should drop a hammer on my toe. Make it real." She looks around, maybe for something heavy, like she's seriously considering injury.

Before I can answer, Mrs. Johnson, her face redder than Miss Sister's streamers, steps away from the crowd. Clutching her program and her big pocketbook, she storms across the parking lot. My uncle moves closer to the oleander bush. Who wouldn't choose taking a chance on a prickly rash over facing Mrs. Johnson up close? I pretend I'm a statue. It doesn't work.

"Anabel? What's going on? What are *they* doing here?" Mrs. Johnson glares at me and my uncle. When she finally stops huffing, she notices the bandage. "Oh dear. What happened?"

"Bruised my foot a little." Anabel takes two wobbly steps back, then says, "Actually, Mom, it's fine. It's an excuse." Leaning down, she slowly unravels the yards of white gauze.

"An excuse? You couldn't dance that one flapper number? All those hours spent sewing feathers and tassels wasted?" Mrs. Johnson's shoulders and huge hat droop and her high heels sink into the dirt.

"I planned to explain to you and Daddy. Later. Didn't think you'd come at five o'clock."

Mrs. Johnson touches a fake purple flower on her fancy blouse and takes a deep, sad breath. "I missed seeing my only child perform." She narrows her eyes and says, "Did he have something to do with this? I thought we talked about *inappropriate friends*, Anabel."

I should be hurrying to the Rest Easy where I belong. No matter what my uncle plans to say to me, it can't be as bad as listening to Mrs. Johnson. But Uncle Raymond moves closer, stepping between me and Mrs. Johnson. Before he can answer, Anabel's right in front of her mom, firmly planting her hands on her hips.

"If you're talking about Theo, he didn't even know," she says.

Just a little white lie. And actually, I *didn't* know she'd show up in shorts and a bandage on recital day, caught red-handed.

Anabel grabs my wrist. Her voice gets louder. "It's not polite to say that about him. He's my *good* friend."

Wow! Chills run up my arm even though it's ninety-eight degrees out here. Anabel opens her mouth to say something else nice about me, I'm sure. But Miss Sister's waltzing over to us now. "Why, Raymond Gary, you came!" He clutches his cap. Miss Sister keeps talking. "Did you enjoy our recital? Wasn't Theo's music the icing on the cake?" She looks at Anabel and winks. "How's that foot, dearie? Think you'll be able to dance on it soon? Or maybe run a few bases?"

"We were just discussing her injury," Mrs. Johnson says. "And her future as a dancer."

"Mom, nobody in the history of softball players has ever been one of those ballerina people you think I can be. Next year, I'll be on the school team. Lots of practices." She stares straight at her mother, her voice steady. "Dancing lessons are over."

"Over? Not forever, of course. I know what's best. Dancing will make you graceful."

"Dream on, Mom," Anabel practically shouts. Now parents and kids pouring out of the auditorium make a huge circle to walk around us. "This is not gonna work. I don't care about being graceful. No dancing. Ever." She tosses the bandage, barely missing Mrs. Johnson.

"Ballroom dancing could be fun," I joke under my breath. In case Anabel heard me, I take a step back.

Mrs. Johnson heard me all right. "Miss Sister, you need to be careful of who you let stay at the Rest Easy. I don't appreciate thievery."

"Nothing was stolen." Miss Sister faces Anabel's mother and says quietly, "The money was misplaced, and it turned up. That's that."

I chew on my lip, hold tight to my good-luck coin, and slide closer to my uncle. But my heart's beating faster than the hat dance song. If anybody can save this day, it's Miss Sister.

She glances at Mrs. Johnson, then takes Anabel's hand. "Dear, your future is as a softball player."

"Thanks, Miss Sister," Anabel says.

Mrs. Johnson's shoulders sag even deeper. "Are you sure about this?"

Anabel rolls her eyes at me and glares at her mother. "We'll talk about dancing at home, Mom. Or rather, *not* dancing."

Mrs. Johnson slips her arm around Anabel's waist to help her hobble off. With a broken toe. Which doesn't exist. I've heard enough about Anabel and her toe to last three lifetimes.

Once they've disappeared, Uncle Raymond finally speaks. "That woman believes she can boss the world." He shakes his head, then turns to Miss Sister. "Thanks for taking up for me. Not sure I deserved that."

"You made things right, Raymond. It was all a misunderstanding."

"Can we help carry something back to the Rest Easy?" he asks. "Me and Theo are good for that."

When we finish packing up the fake palm tree and her record albums, and every bit of crepe paper's off the stage, Miss Sister says, "Almost time for supper. See you back home." She squeezes her tiny self into her packed car and drives off. Tucking record albums under my arm and a paper flower in my pocket, I start toward the Rest Easy. Before I'm out of the parking lot, Uncle Raymond stops me.

"Wait up, son. Almost forgot." He hands me an envelope, then quickly heads back to the auditorium for flowers and streamers.

I open it. A card. With birds and trees and a bright round sun and a corny verse about having a beautiful day. My fingers trace the handwriting across the bottom. All my uncle's written is

LOVE, RAYMOND T. GARY

I'm about ten feet taller than I was when I woke up this morning. Being mad at my uncle felt good for a little while. It feels better when I stop being mad. If I didn't think Anabel or even Mamie might see me, I'd skip all the way to the Rest Easy.

CHAPTER TWENTY-SEVEN

The Way to Stay in Destiny

Even after we've hauled every fake palm tree into the Rest Easy's attic, the piano problem hangs in the air like a storm cloud. But a plan is playing out in my head. It's gotta be perfect. By the time a lizard scoots down one table leg and back up another, I've figured it out. But will Uncle Raymond agree?

Careful not to trip on the rose-colored carpet still loose on one side, I take the stairs two at a time. This is my house now. I know exactly which frayed edges to step over. When I open our bedroom door, I see my uncle's pulled out his beat-up army duffel. The one he dragged all the way from Alaska to Kentucky and now Florida.

Uncle Raymond starts talking. "Here's the thing. I see you love playing the piano. You're good. I heard you. But I can't live someplace with all this music."

"Because it reminds you of your family? Your sister?" I ask.

He nods. "Maybe one of these days that'll be a happy memory. So far, it ain't."

"So, you're going?" I ask.

Uncle Raymond stops stuffing T-shirts into his bag and rubs the faded stenciling across the side: *Sergeant Raymond Gary.* After a while, he says, "Gotta take that job in Mount Flora."

"You don't *gotta* do anything," I answer. "If you don't want to."

He shakes his head. "I won't say if I go, you go. But I don't know what else to do. We need to stick together."

Moving his duffel so I can sit right next to him, I say, "I have an idea. I'll stay here with Miss Sister while you try out the new job. Come back on your days off. I checked the bus. It's not hard. When you're at the Rest Easy, I'll try to keep away from the piano. Or play so quiet you can't hear."

From the way Uncle Raymond's mouth twitches, I hope he's working it out in his head. "Seems you've thought hard about this," he says.

"Our favorite baseball player, Hank Aaron — he had to be apart from his family. When he wasn't much older than me." I take a deep breath and wait.

My uncle smiles at Aaron's name. "What's Miss Sister think?" he asks.

Miss Sister doesn't know about my plan. Uncle Raymond needed to hear it first.

"She'll think it's a good idea," I say hopefully. "I'll have my piano, but you don't have to hear."

"Bet they have music classes over in Mount Flora. You could play at school. Much bigger school there." He's trying to convince both of us.

"Miss Sister's a plenty good piano teacher." For a minute the room seems crowded, like there's not enough air or enough light. But it's my room now. I'm not leaving. I'm not the one deciding to take off.

"If Miss Sister agrees, you can give it a try. At least till school starts." Uncle Raymond looks right at me. "I reckon we're doing okay, aren't we, boy?"

Sure, now that I have a plan, I'm okay. Slipping my hand in my shorts pocket, I pull out my good-luck piece. "Maybe you want this back?"

"Naw, son. That's yours to keep," he answers and closes my palm around his old guitar pick.

I squeeze that quarter all the way downstairs, not sure which one of us needs luck the most.

After supper, I sit on the porch listening to the crickets until Miss Sister comes out. "You did yourself proud today, Theo. Best music I ever had!" she says.

"Thanks," I tell her. "For letting me be in the recital." Even though I'm about to explode inside, I say slowly, "Got something to ask you."

"Go ahead, ask away," she answers, pushing the creaky glider back and forth.

"My uncle told you about his job in Mount Flora. But the Rest Easy's my home now. Destiny's where I want to live. If I have to leave with him, I'll miss Anabel. Maybe even Mamie. Well, maybe not Mamie. The truth is, I'd mostly miss you." Once I get started, the words spill over each other like that thing Miss Sister taught me, an arpeggio, one note after another. "Can I stay at the Rest Easy while Uncle Raymond goes back and forth? At least this summer. By school time, September, maybe something will be different."

"Don't even have to think twice, honey. It would be a joy. If Raymond approves. You two are both stubborn as mules." When she raises an eyebrow at me, I smile so big my face might crack open.

"My uncle says it's okay for now. He could decide he hates

the job and he could change his mind about hearing my music. Maybe I'll even be ready to leave after the summer."

Maybe, but I don't think I'll ever want to leave here.

"Right now, you need a steady riverbank to come home to. Destiny and the Rest Easy seem just about right." Miss Sister points to the row of pillows, their curlicued lessons lined up on the glider. "Time heals just about anything, Theo," she says.

A lot of time went by since Uncle Raymond stopped loving his only sister, and nothing healed. A lot of time since he came back from that war, but he hasn't forgotten who ridiculed him. But really, since he met me, not that much time's passed. Already he likes me more than when we stepped onto that bus in Kentucky.

"I told him you'll help with my piano and I'll play for your classes."

"Tiny details! Easy to work out," she says. "Just watch where you throw that baseball. My toolshed's taking a beating." Miss Sister rattles the melting ice in her sweet tea and laughs. Fanning herself with a paper fan decorated with roses, she says, "Don't know why anybody lives in Florida in the summer. Just too hot to breathe."

Since the ceiling fan on the front porch moves the air a little bit, we sit together waiting for Uncle Raymond till the cuckoo clock announces seven thirty. I'd almost forgotten! *Anabel!*

When my uncle steps onto the porch, we nearly knock each other flat down. "Whoa, son. Where you off to in such a hurry?" he says.

"Can I meet Anabel at the ice-cream stand? To celebrate the end of school. And the end of her dance career." Miss Sister and I laugh out loud at the exact same minute.

"Be back before the streetlights come on," he says. "Nighttime's —"

I interrupt. "The worst time for getting in trouble. You told me that once or twice." This time his stupid rule makes me smile. I skip down the front steps, not caring who sees me now.

At the end of the sidewalk, I hear a tune drifting down from the porch. I swear it's my uncle whistling the "Glow Worm" song.

CHAPTER TWENTY-EIGHT

Big Wishes

I run all the way to Main Street. Before I even catch my breath, Anabel's talking. "First off, I'm sorry. About the way my mother acted."

"I bet she loves me now. If she heard what I said about ballroom dancing, she might sign us up for lessons." Okay, that was pretty funny. Me and Anabel, dancing together. Anabel doesn't laugh.

When we step up to the window and order, I stare up at the big awning painted with flamingos, seashells, a little boy eating ice cream. "'Best Ice Cream and Sno-Cones in Destiny, Florida. The Town Time Forgot.' Weird town motto, huh?"

"Ha. The town *everybody and everything* forgot," she says, slurping her ice cream. "I bet not even baseball players remember living here."

"Maybe I'll write to Henry Aaron. See if he wants his tackle box back." I wipe bright orange sno-cone drips off my hand and onto my shorts.

"You know, Theo, we may not have famous baseball players strolling around Destiny anymore, but I had fun figuring it out."

Saying nothing, I blush a color that matches my sno-cone.

She reaches into her knapsack. "Almost forgot. Brought you something. Kind of an if-you-go-away and thank-you thing."

Nobody gives me gifts. Well, not since my uncle took over.

"It's Henry Aaron's baseball for sure," she says, handing me the ball from our Destiny Day display. "You saw where he'd tossed it against Miss Sister's shed."

I shake my head.

"Well, it *could* have been his."

I turn the ball over. Who knows? Maybe it did belong to Hammerin' Hank Aaron. "Thanks, Anabel, but guess what. I'm not leaving. I figured out a way to stay in Destiny." I offer her the ball.

"Keep it," she says, pushing it toward me. "So what are we doing this summer?"

"I'll work on my piano playing. Miss Sister's letting me help with her classes. Don't suppose you'll be signing up for advanced tap? Maybe toe dancing?" I do a little dance just to show her how great it could be.

"Very funny." She laughs but doesn't attempt a shuffle-ball-change. "Wonder how you can sneak out from practicing the piano to play baseball."

Anabel has no clue.

"Maybe you'll teach me to surf this summer?" I ask.

Before she can answer, a shiny black car stops across the street. All four windows slide down. A tall, skinny guy steps out and saunters up to the ice-cream window, his back to us.

"Nobody here drives a car that fancy," Anabel says.

We move close enough to hear him order. "Two orange sno-cones, with cream topping. One plain vanilla milk shake. To go." He carries the cardboard tray to the car, gets in, and they drive slowly toward the highway out of town.

Grabbing my hand, Anabel steps off the sidewalk and stares. "Theo! Did you see that license plate? I think it said Georgia HLA 715. It's Henry Aaron! Back in town to check out the Rest Easy!"

"Anabel, you are totally out to lunch."

"Wow! Wish he'd shown up earlier. Hank Aaron! At our Baseball History in Destiny booth."

"We would have gotten a zillion extra-credit points," I joke. "We'll never know."

She smiles and heads down the street. "See you tomorrow?" she calls back.

"Sure. The beach? Teach me body surfing?"

I don't have a clue what I'm talking about, but I'm making my wishes big.

CHAPTER TWENTY-NINE

Theo's Dream

*W*hen I get to the Rest Easy, Uncle Raymond's waiting on the front porch. As the stars pop out, he points to the sky. "Big Dipper. Almost as pretty as in Alaska." If he's decided there's something in Florida *almost as good* as his memories, my uncle might be coming around. "Maybe rain's not threatening after all," he says.

"What's that thing about weather in Destiny?" I ask, remembering Mr. Dawson's jokes. "Blink and it changes. Kind of like my life these days, come to think about it."

Uncle Raymond laughs. I'll never get used to hearing that sound.

When Miss Sister comes out, I say, "Thank you for letting me stay here while my uncle sees about his new job."

"Wouldn't have it any other way. I picture great things for you, honey." She sinks into her white rocking chair and swishes her paper fan back and forth, hardly stirring up the air. "Speaking of greatness, why don't you go inside and tickle my ivories for a bit?"

My uncle stands up quick, running away from my music. But in the faint light of the porch lamp, I see Miss Sister wink and wave her jangly bracelets to shoo me off. Just because he can't bear to hear doesn't mean I can't play quietly to myself.

Inside the dance studio, I open the big window. Next to it is my favorite of Miss Sister's sayings: *Music Makes Memories,* under a picture of a little girl dancing in her tutu with her grandmother.

A tiny breeze drifts in from the porch, and memories and music hop in my head to the beat of Miss Sister's rocking chair thump-thump-thumping. Uncle Raymond's there, too, his long legs stretched across the bottom step, as far from the window as he can get. But at least he's still out there.

When I sit on the piano bench, my toes reach for the shiny pedal on the right. Miss Sister told me that pedal holds the notes. Maybe they'll drift through the front hall to Mr. and Mrs. Hernandez clinking checkers on the board in the dining room. Then sneak quietly under the porch where Ginger Rogers keeps cool. Even to Mamie's room — if she promises not to sing along off-key.

I decide on a hymn my grandma and I sang back in Kentucky, "Rock of Ages." Uncle Raymond told me he and my mama were in the choir together. Maybe he remembers this one.

Stretching up to the sky, then wiggling my fingers, I send the melody quietly flowing from the piano keys to the front porch. I mix in two black notes — F-sharp, B-flat. Everything pours out perfectly, fitting together like on Mr. Monk's record album. I'm calling this song "Theo's Dream."

ACKNOWLEDGMENTS

Music and dance connections seem to tap into my life at just the right time. A special nod to my childhood friend Sandra, dancer extraordinaire, and also to Barbara, who showed me all the right moves, from tap to the Twist. The character of Miss Sister is based partially on my own very special dance teacher, Ruth Hart, and on the stories I heard growing up in Cleveland, Mississippi, from the students of Kathlyn "Sister" Cockersole and her mother, Ruth Keywood. For all the dancers and pianists who've inspired me with your art, your music, and your words, a huge thanks.

To the entire team at Scholastic, your choreography leaps off the pages of my books. An enthusiastic *Brava!* goes to my editor, the wise and funny Andrea Davis Pinkney.

Linda Pratt, my talented agent, challenged me to make this book the best it could be. Many, many thanks for your generosity, skill, and patience. Especially patience.

Without my critique groups, Theo might still be languishing in his room at the Rest Easy, surrounded by all the wrong people. He first came to life from a writing prompt thrown out by my longtime friend, Leslie Guccione. Another writer, Teddie Aggeles, helped this story grow in many ways, including remembering the color of her cafeteria trays. Near what I thought was the novel's end, my longtime critique partner, Janet McLaughlin, read Theo's tarot cards and kept me from taking a misstep.

Stories begin with questions, and answers turn up in unexpected places. For many reasons and many answers, I'm fortunate to be surrounded by SCBWI members, especially those in my new home state of Florida.

Like performing, writing requires practice. An enthusiastic audience makes the long preparation worth every minute. To my friends and family who encourage me, you know who you are. I know I am eternally grateful.

ABOUT THE AUTHOR

Augusta Scattergood is the author of *Glory Be*, a National Public Radio Backseat Book Club selection, a Texas Bluebonnet Award nominee, and a novel hailed by Newbery medalist Richard Peck as the story of a bygone era "beautifully recalled." A children's book reviewer and former librarian, Ms. Scattergood has devoted her life and career to getting books into the hands of young readers. Her reviews and articles regularly appear in *The Christian Science Monitor*, *Delta Magazine*, and other publications. Ms. Scattergood, who lives in St. Petersburg, Florida, and Madison, New Jersey, is an avid blogger. To learn more about her and her books, please visit www.ascattergood.com.